For Love
of
Christy

Books by Jasmine Cresswell

For Love of Christy

of

Christy

Jasmine Cresswell

SPEAKING VOLUMES, LLC

NAPLES, FLORIDA

2012

For Love of Christy

Originally published under the name Jasmine Craig

ISBN 978-1-61232-813-3

Chapter One

LAURA TURNED THE squad car onto Colfax Avenue and headed back toward police headquarters. The girl with the spiked purple hair was still standing outside the Galaxy Video Arcade, leaning against one of the entrance pillars and doing her best to look casual. She wore skin-tight jeans topped by an oversized black sweat shirt, and a nylon backpack rested on the pavement at her feet. Thick layers of makeup failed to conceal the fact that she was pale, tired, and somewhat dirty. She was also thin, without much curve at the breast or hips, so that she might have been any age between twelve and eighteen. To Laura's experienced eye, everything about her shrieked *runaway*.

The Galaxy was a favorite hangout for high school dropouts, and it was crowded with young people, but for once nobody seemed to be fighting. Laura spotted Samson Jones, leader of Denver's largest youth gang, as he emerged from the shadows of a narrow alleyway alongside the arcade. He strutted toward the purple-

1

haired girl, his neck chains glinting in the late afternoon sunshine, and dropped one hand casually onto her hip as he began to speak to her. Purple Hair didn't seem to like what he was saying and she grabbed her backpack, darting with lightning speed into the arcade. Samson scowled, hesitated for a moment, and then ran after her.

Laura slammed the squad car to a halt alongside the curb, vaulting over the passenger seat and joining the chase. Purple Hair headed straight for the rear of the arcade, her movements clumsy with panic as she dodged around a group of shaven-headed youths with safety pins stuck through their ears. Out of the corner of her eye, Laura saw Samson slip through a side door, but she didn't bother to pursue him. At this moment she was more interested in helping the young runaway.

Purple Hair didn't make it very far. She stumbled against a beefy young man who was trying to save the world from alien invaders and accidentally knocked the joystick out of his hand.

"Don't you got no eyes?" he yelled, letting rip with a string of obscenities. "I had my highest score ever, you stupid little bitch!"

"Let go of the girl," Laura said quietly. "Right now."

The youth jerked around, his clenched fists ready to swing, but he changed his mind when he saw who was speaking. Laura was only five feet five and probably less than two-thirds of his weight, but a police uniform was a powerful persuader. He grunted his disgust, shoved the runaway hard against the video machine, and walked off to conquer another make-believe universe.

"I'm Sergeant Forbes of the Denver Police Department," Laura told the girl, showing her badge. "Are you all right?"

"Y-yes thank you. I'm fine. Terrific." The girl was visibly shaking, but she tossed her head defiantly and began to walk away when she saw that Samson was no longer pursuing her.

Laura grabbed the girl's arm and propelled her firmly in the direction of the main exit. "We have to talk," she said, raising her voice to be heard above the mega-decibel level of the recorded rock music. "Come with me, please. The noise in here will deafen us both if we stay much longer."

The girl complied with evident reluctance. "Thanks for your help," she said as soon as they reached the squad car. "I guess I'll be leaving now."

"Not quite yet. Get in the car, please. I have some questions to ask you."

The girl's face went chalk white beneath her streaky makeup. "I d-don't want to get into a police car. Why do I have to? I haven't done anything wrong."

"Perhaps not, but I need to ask you a few questions and I'm already late in going off duty, so don't make things difficult, okay?"

Purple Hair's brief moment of defiance seemed to dissipate into sheer weariness, and she sank into the passenger seat, huddling her backpack in her arms. Laura got into the car, checked the rearview mirror, then edged into the heavy stream of oncoming traffic. "You nearly found yourself in a heap of trouble back there at the arcade," she remarked. "Samson doesn't like girls who defy him."

"Samson?"

"The guy with the neck chains."

"Oh." Purple Hair looked down, then shrugged her shoulders in a pathetic attempt to appear sophisticated. "It was no big deal. He wanted me . . . he wanted me to . . ."

Her voice trailed away and Laura didn't press her to continue. She could guess exactly what Samson had wanted. "What's your name?" she asked gently. "And where do you live?"

There was a long silence before the girl replied. "My name's Christy Logan," she muttered finally.

"And do you live in the Denver area, Christy?"

"Not . . . not exactly."

Definitely a runaway, Laura concluded, taking care to let none of her sympathy show in her stern expression. "Did you know that it's a federal offense for a young person under eighteen to leave home without the permission of her legal guardians?"

"A federal offense? You mean—like I could go to jail?"

"You could be sent to a juvenile group home, yes."

"Well, that's no problem, because . . . because I'm eighteen already."

The poor kid was fourteen maximum, probably less, Laura decided. Five years of experience as a police officer had made her an expert at assessing the age and background of runaways, and despite the street-smart purple hair, Christy seemed naive in many ways. Seen up close, the layers of makeup couldn't disguise the childlike softness of her features, just as the baggy sweat shirt couldn't conceal the coltish immaturity of her body.

Laura didn't waste time disputing Christy's claim that she was eighteen. "Please show me some identification," she said politely. "And also some proof that you have sufficient funds to support yourself. Even eighteen-year-olds can be arrested on vagrancy charges, you know."

There was a long pause. "I don't have any identification," Christy whispered finally. "My . . . my purse was stolen."

"I'm sorry, because if you don't have proof that you're an adult, I have to rely on my own judgment. And my judgment as a police officer tells me that you're less than eighteen and not a legal resident of the state of Colorado."

Christy gulped, clutching her arms around her skinny

body. "Does that mean you won't . . . you won't let me go?"

"I'm afraid it means just that." Laura drove the squad car into the police parking lot and cut the ignition. "Time to get out of the car, Christy. I'm going off duty, so I'll have to hand you over to one of the detectives in the juvenile division."

"Are you arres—" Christy stuttered, unable to say the threatening word. She swallowed hard, then tried again. "Are you arresting me?" she asked.

"Not arresting you," Laura corrected softly. "Taking you into protective custody. Out of the car, Christy."

The girl looked pleadingly at Laura. "Don't arrest me," she said huskily. "I'm only trying to find my father. I came here to see if he would let me stay with him for a while."

Laura felt a surge of pity as she looked at the vulnerable young face in front of her. If Christy was like most other runaways, she probably hadn't heard from her father in months, and yet she had hitchhiked for miles hoping that he would welcome her into his home. If she could read the grim statistics on parental rejection in the police department files, Laura thought sadly, the poor kid wouldn't be so optimistic.

"Are your parents divorced?" she asked, although she already guessed the answer.

Christy nodded tersely.

"And you've been living with your mother?"

"Yes, in San Diego." The girl's mouth twisted with curiously adult bitterness. "But my mother travels a lot."

"Denver's a long way from San Diego. You must have been on the road for a while."

She shrugged. "A couple of days."

More like a week, Laura thought, looking at the girl's travel-stained clothes and exhausted features.

"Your mother must be worried about you. Why don't we go inside the station so that you can give her a call?"

Christy's gray eyes shuttered into total coldness. "My mother won't be home. Please, Sergeant, I really want to stay here in Denver. Isn't there some way you could help me get in touch with my father?"

"Maybe. But if your mother has custody rights, she has to give her permission before I can do anything. I need her phone number, Christy."

"My dad has custody rights as well, I know he has. It was the only way he would agree to pay my mother alimony."

"If your dad has custody rights, then how come you don't know how to get in touch with him?" Laura touched the girl's skinny arm. "Christy, have you faced up to the fact that your dad may not want to see you?"

Her eyes blazed passionately. "Of course he wants to see me. My mother keeps me away from him just to make him mad. She won't let me see him, or talk to him on the phone, or *anything.*"

Laura barely suppressed a sigh. The fantasy of an eager father, desperate to find his missing child, was one nurtured by many rejected children. She knew that if she had the sense she was born with, she'd march the child upstairs to the juvenile division, and hand her straight over to one of the detectives. Unfortunately, her common sense had never been a match for her sympathy toward the underdogs of the world, and she hated to think of the poor kid locked up in a detention center while a battery of state officials pondered her fate.

Cursing herself for a sentimental fool, Laura reached into the squad car and picked up her clipboard. Her brothers always claimed that under her starched police uniform beat the heart of an oversized marshmallow. Christy wasn't the first runaway to spend the night in Laura's small apartment, and she almost certainly wouldn't be the last.

"Come into the station with me while I check out for the day," she said resignedly. "Then we'll take my car and see if we can find your father."

For the first time since Laura had met her, Christy smiled—an enchanting smile that gave her face an odd, haunting illusion of familiarity. "Thank you, Sergeant, thanks a million!" She skipped up the stairs, bounding from step to step like an eager puppy. "I know we can find my dad if we just drive around a bit."

"It's past six o'clock already," Laura commented, glancing at her watch. She logged in the return of the squad car and handed over the keys to the duty officer. "If we're going to find your father tonight, we'd better get busy. You don't know his home address, but do you know the name of the company where he works?"

"He doesn't exactly work in Denver," Christy said, shifting uneasily from one foot to the other.

"He works in the suburbs, you mean? Aurora, maybe?"

"No. He's not . . . I don't think he's working right now. He's kind of on vacation. You know, taking a rest."

Great, Laura thought, closing her locker with a decided thump. Wonderful. The kid's hitchhiked a thousand miles to get away from a mother who's never home, so that she can join up with a father who was "taking a rest" from gainful employment. She called good night to the duty officer and ushered Christy out into the parking lot.

"Never mind," she said, sounding a great deal more cheerful than she felt. "If you don't know the name of his employer, do you know the general area where he lives?"

Christy's expression brightened. "I'm sure I could find his house if we drove around for a while, although it's four years since I was there. I tried to get a taxi to take me this afternoon, but the drivers all said I had to pay them first and I don't have any money. The house is somewhere off of Hampden Avenue, and you can see the Rocky Mountains from the backyard."

"That should help a lot," Laura said dryly. "Hampden Avenue only stretches for thirty miles, and there can't be more than a half million homes in Denver with a view of the mountains."

Christy giggled as she got into Laura's battered Ford Pinto. "Dad lives in Cherry Hills. That's not too big an area, is it? Could we try to find the house before it gets too dark?"

"I guess we can," Laura said, suppressing a feeling of surprise. Cherry Hills was one of Denver's most exclusive suburbs and even the smaller houses there tended to be outrageously expensive. Christy's father might be unemployed at the moment, but at some time or another he must have had a well-paying job.

Laura drove onto the highway and Christy chattered happily about her previous visit to Denver. The highlight of her stay had apparently been a white-water rafting trip down the rapids of the Colorado River.

"Did your mother come rafting with you and your dad?" Laura asked.

"Are you kidding? She just went shopping all the time. Sometimes I think that if they closed all the stores for twenty-four hours, she'd go completely crazy."

Glancing over, Laura saw Christy's scornful expression. "Face facts," she said quietly. "You may not enjoy living with your mother right now, but that doesn't mean all your problems would be solved if you moved in with your dad. There are worse faults than liking shopping, you know."

"Yeah," Christy said. "Tell me about them." She hunched her shoulders defiantly and stared out of the car window.

Laura sighed, braking at the traffic lights that marked

the intersection of Colorado Boulevard with Hampden Avenue. She gestured toward a church with soaring stained-glass windows.

"We're approaching the boundaries of Cherry Hills, Christy. Do any of these buildings look familiar?"

Christy nibbled anxiously on her lip. "Not very, and it's beginning to get kind of dark."

"Don't worry, we still have at least another hour of daylight." Laura turned west and a tense silence filled the car until Christy suddenly swiveled around in her seat.

"That was it, that was the road!" she exclaimed. "You have to go back there to the traffic lights and turn right! Quick, Sergeant! Stop now!"

Laura obediently pulled into a side street and reversed their direction. Christy bounced feverishly in her seat, bursting with sudden confidence. "You need to turn right again here," she said, pointing to a narrow, private road, half-hidden behind massive stone pillars and overhanging spruce trees. "Fantastic, this is it! We've found my dad's street! I knew we could do it!"

The road she indicated wound between scattered houses that varied in size between the enormous and the positively palatial. Christy almost jumped out of her seat belt when they finally drove past a gray stone-and-timber house, dimly visible at the end of a long, shrub-bordered driveway. "That's it!" she shrieked. "We're here! This is where my dad lives."

The house was only slightly smaller than Laura's entire apartment building, and the grounds looked better maintained than the botanical gardens. Laura swallowed hard.

"Are you *quite* sure this is your father's house, Christy?"

"Positive." She beamed. "Hurry up, Sergeant. Oh,

boy, I can't wait to see my dad's face when he opens the door! Is he ever going to be surprised!"

He was going to be surprised all right, Laura thought, and she hoped for Christy's sake that the encounter turned out to be everything the child was dreaming of. But there were some practical details to be taken care of before Christy's fairy tale could have a happy ending. Laura would need to see the divorce decree that gave Christy's father custody privileges, otherwise she could be setting up the police department —and herself—for a very nasty scene with Christy's mother.

She drove over a speed bump and slowly edged her seven-year-old Ford onto the curving driveway. She wondered if such plebeian wheels had ever before sullied its pristine surface. As if to answer her question, she rounded a bend and found her progress blocked by a blue Mercedes and a silver Jaguar, which were parked neatly in front of the forbidding, brass-studded door. Although dusk had not yet turned into night, spotlights kept the exterior of the building brilliantly lit, and Laura's professional eye noted the existence of the very latest in electronic security systems.

Christy immediately began to unbuckle her seat belt. "Hey, wait a minute!" Laura said, grabbing her hand. "Before we go banging on the door, you'd better tell me your father's name."

Christy turned a radiant smile in Laura's direction. "It's Ben Logan," she said, and laughed joyfully. "My dad's name is Bennett Logan."

The silence inside the small Ford was deafening. "Bennett Logan?" Laura queried at last.

Christy had the grace to look embarrassed. "Er . . . yes."

"The Bennett Logan?"

"I—um—guess so. I'm sorry I didn't tell you before, but I thought you might not believe me. I was afraid you might think I was making it all up and refuse to help me."

"Hmm. I guess you do look a little bit like him, especially when you smile."

"Do you think so?" Christy flushed with pleasure. "He's fantastically good-looking, don't you think?"

"Yes." Laura drew in a deep breath, squaring her shoulders as she got out of the car. Just because she was about to meet her fantasy lover, the star of *Empire*, the man who set millions of female hearts fluttering each Thursday night, that was no good reason for her palms to start sweating and her knees to begin wobbling. She was a sensible, twenty-seven-year-old woman, for heaven's sake, not a susceptible teenager. She prided herself on being a sturdy pillar of Denver's police force, shortly in line for promotion to detective, provided she didn't screw up. What she needed right now was a little less starry-eyed hero worship and a little more sober professionalism.

Her stern lecture didn't have the spine-stiffening effect it should have, and she tugged nervously at her shirt collar. She wished that she could look cool and dignified instead of hot and flustered. She wished it hadn't been thirteen hours since she got up that morning and applied her usual scanty amount of makeup. She wished she was sleek and glamorous instead of curly-haired and wholesome. She wished . . .

Her mouth curved into a rueful, self-mocking smile as she escorted Christy toward the massive front door. If only her brothers could see her now, she thought, and her smile deepened. Here she was, wondering what it would be like to vamp the man whom the popular press had recently declared the sexiest male in America—and she was the girl who had reached her senior year in high school before any of the boys had noticed she was actually female!

She laughed silently at her own foolishness, then tossed back her soft brown curls and held out her hand. "Come on, Christy," she said, taking the remaining stairs two at a time. "Let's ring the doorbell and find out if your dad's home."

Chapter Two

"COME ON IN, Ronnie, we weren't expecting you so soo—" The smartly dressed, immaculately coiffed woman who had opened the door broke off her welcome in mid-sentence, not attempting to conceal her distaste for the unexpected appearance of a uniformed police officer and a scruffy teenager standing side by side on Bennett Logan's imposing front doorstep.

"May I help you?" she inquired coldly.

"I hope so," Laura responded, drawing herself up to her full five feet five inches and resisting the impulse to give her uniform another twitch. She extended her official identification. "I'm Sergeant Forbes of the Denver Police Department, and I'd like to speak to Mr. Bennett Logan, if he's at home."

The young woman was not impressed by Laura's badge of office. "Mr. Logan never sees visitors without an appointment," she said, preparing to close the door.

"This is official police business."

The woman hesitated, her gaze skimming assessingly

over Laura's uniform. "Maybe I can help you, Sergeant. I'm Prudence Datscher, Mr. Logan's personal private secretary."

Christy gave a sudden, mischievous giggle. "And I'm Christy Logan, his daughter," she said. "Could you take us to see him, please?"

"His daughter!" Prudence Datscher's calm facade finally cracked and she stared at Christy in stunned, incredulous silence. She quickly recovered her poise, however, and stepped back, gesturing to indicate that they should follow.

"You'd better come into my office, both of you, while I check this out. Follow me, please." She led them briskly through a huge, cathedral-ceilinged foyer into a pleasantly decorated room, equipped with a computer system, a large desk piled high with papers, and several comfortable chairs.

"Please take a seat," she said, but Christy ignored the secretary's instructions and ran out into the foyer. The murmur of a man's voice drifted out of a half-open door at the end of the hallway and she gave a squeak of excitement as she dashed toward the back of the house.

"Daddy, it's me!" she yelled, pushing open the door. "I came here to Denver to find you! Mom wants more money and she was going to take me to Canada to live, so I ran away when she went to New York with Eric, and Sergeant Forbes is a policewoman and she helped me to find you!"

Laura and the secretary caught up with Christy just as the tall, blond man seated behind the desk rose to his feet, dropping the script he had been reading and overturning a chair in his haste to reach Christy's side. His blue eyes—the darkest blue Laura had ever seen—blazed with emotion as he strode across the room and swept his daughter into his arms.

"Oh, God, sweetheart, it's been so long! How are you, honey? How did you get here? When did you arrive in Denver? Damn, but it's good to see you, sweetheart. I've been trying to find you for so long!"

"It's good to see you, too, Dad. I've missed you so much!"

They hugged each other in silence for several minutes, then Christy sniffed and leaned back, gazing up at her father provocatively. "Do you see how much I've grown? I'm five feet three inches already."

"Ten more inches and we'll be twins."

Christy giggled. "What about my hairstyle? Do you like it? Mom can't stand it."

Laura could see that Bennett Logan was still too dazed to absorb the full impact of his daughter's conversation, but he grinned affectionately and ruffled his fingers through the stiff purple spikes framing Christy's elfin features. "It's a great hairstyle," he said. "Purple's my favorite color, especially for hair. In fact, I think you look terrific all over." He dropped a kiss on her forehead. "I even like that strange black stuff you have stuck all over your eyelids, although I think you might look better without it."

Christy wrinkled her nose. "It's a special sort of mascara, but maybe it's smudged because I haven't washed for ages, and I guess I kind of started crying when I found out my purse was stolen." Her breath suddenly caught in an awkward little sob, and her brittle gaiety crumbled. "Oh Dad, it took me such a long time to find you! I arrived in Denver yesterday but I had no money and the operator wouldn't give me your phone number because it's unlisted, so I couldn't call you. If it hadn't been for Sergeant Forbes nearly arresting me, I don't think I'd ever have gotten here."

His expression was grim as he pulled her into his arms and stroked her gently on the shoulders. "You're safe now, honey," he said softly. "You're here with me and, believe me, this time I'm not letting you go. *No-*

body can take you away now that I have you home again."

Christy knuckled her eyes, trying to stop her tears. "I don't have to go back and live with . . . her?"

Bennett's mouth tightened into a harsh line. "No, and that's a promise, Christy. You won't have to live with your mother ever again, unless you choose to."

"I'm glad," she said simply. "Mom doesn't like me much, you know." She yawned, her tears stopping as she nestled contentedly against his chest. "Dad, did I introduce you to Sergeant Laura Forbes? She didn't arrest me, even though she thought I was a vagrant. She drove me all around Cherry Hills, so that we could look for your house. I'd never have found you without her help."

Bennett Logan's head snapped up and he looked directly at Laura for the first time since she'd entered the room. Heat flared beneath her skin as she met the full impact of his powerful gaze. She suddenly knew exactly what the television critics meant when they talked about his sexual charisma. Her surroundings faded away, leaving her aware of nothing save the compelling force of his dark blue eyes—and the tiny curl of excitement unwinding deep in the pit of her stomach. After a moment of silent scrutiny he smiled, and her throat went dry.

"It seems that I'm very deeply in your debt, Sergeant," he said in the husky voice that kept millions of female viewers tuned into *Empire* each week. "I've been searching for Christy for nearly four years, and I can't tell you what it means to have her home with me at last. I can only thank you for your kindness. I suspect that if some other police officer had found her, Christy and I wouldn't be together right now."

His smile was sexy enough to charm the socks off any female still breathing, and his warm, appreciative gaze seemed to have been expressly designed to melt a woman's bones. Laura told herself that a police officer's bones ought to be immune to melting, but her body didn't seem to be listening.

She finally managed to tear her gaze away from his mesmerizing smile and, after a moment or two, her heart stopped trying to turn somersaults. "I'm glad I noticed Christy before she ran into serious trouble," she replied primly. "Police officers always prefer to prevent a disaster instead of waiting around to pick up the pieces afterward." Realizing that she sounded like the chief of detectives giving new recruits a graduating pep talk, she cleared her throat hurriedly. "However, Mr. Logan, there are still a couple of minor details I need to clear up before I can leave you and Christy to enjoy each other's company."

"Do you think maybe we could start making dinner while you two discuss things?" Christy asked anxiously. "It's so long since I ate that my stomach's forgotten what food feels like. I'm definitely going to die of hunger any minute now."

"Perhaps the sergeant would be willing to save you from starvation and continue our talk in the kitchen?" Bennett directed another of his devastating smiles in Laura's direction. "I saw a huge tray of super-deluxe lasagna in the freezer last time I went looking for ice cubes. How does lasagna sound to your empty stomach, sweetheart?"

"Heavenly," Christy said, speeding toward the study door. "And maybe Sergeant Forbes would like to stay and eat dinner with us. She was just going off duty when she found me."

"Of course." Bennett leaned over and began to gather up the scattered pages of his script. "Please, Sergeant, if you feel hungry enough to eat prepackaged, reheated lasagna, you'd be very welcome to join my daughter and me."

She didn't need five years of experience as an investigator to know that Bennett didn't want her to join them for dinner. What's more, she had the oddest feeling that a natural desire to be alone with his daughter wasn't the only reason for his reluctance. Christy, however, had her thoughts set firmly on food and she sensed no subtle nuances in her father's invitation.

"Please stay," she said, her eyes dancing with laughter. "The truth is, Dad and I are both terrible cooks and we're hoping you'll heat the lasagna and save us from disaster."

Prudence Datscher spoke reprovingly. "Sergeant Forbes is a police officer, Christy, not a short-order cook. Besides, I'm here, and I'm quite willing to see that the lasagna doesn't get burned."

Christy blushed scarlet. "I'm really sorry, Sergeant Forbes, I didn't mean to be rude. It was just I knew you were hungry and you seemed like the sort of person who would be a good cook."

Laura had fully intended to refuse Bennett Logan's less-than-gracious invitation, but Christy's embarrassed apology caused her to change her mind. After all, she decided, she could clear up the few outstanding technicalities as easily in the kitchen as in the study. And, darn it, a meal shared with Bennett Logan—even an unwilling Bennett Logan—would be something exciting to look back on, particularly these days when her budget had no room in it for frivolity of any kind. Her brothers' financial situation was so desperate that it had been weeks since she permitted herself the luxury of eating out. Surely there wouldn't be any harm in sitting at the kitchen table and indulging herself in half an hour of harmless fantasy?

She smiled at Christy, avoiding both the reproving frowns of the secretary and the enigmatic blankness of Bennett Logan's profile. "You were right, I enjoy cooking and I'd be delighted to heat up the lasagna, especially since it's one of my favorite meals."

"That's all settled then," Bennett declared, dumping the pages of script onto his desk. He turned around, his expression revealing no trace of its former reluctance, and smiled casually at his secretary. "You've already eaten dinner, haven't you, Pru?"

"Yes, thank you. The housekeeper made me some baked fish before she left for the day."

"Then would you give Ronnie a call and tell him not to bother coming over? I'm obviously not going to finish reading this script tonight, so there's no point in wasting his time. I'm only sorry *you* wasted so much of your evening, hanging around waiting for me. Is it too late for you to catch a movie or something? The keys to the Jaguar are in my desk drawer if you need them."

"Thank you, but I'm reading an excellent biography of Abraham Lincoln, so I think I'll go to my room." Prudence looked down and busied herself with fastening the buttons on her beige linen jacket. When she looked up again, she was smiling brightly. "Anyway, Ben, my evening wasn't wasted. I used the time to catch up on some of your fan mail, and I sent back all those scripts you've already read and rejected."

"I have no idea what I'd do without you," he replied, giving her a quick, impersonal hug as he escorted her to the door of his study. "You're the most organized person I've ever been lucky enough to meet. See you tomorrow, Prudence."

"Yes, good night, Ben." Laura noticed an infinitesimal pause before the secretary added, "Good night, Christy. Welcome home."

"Thanks. Good night Ms. . . . er . . . Ms. Datscher."

"But you must call me Prudence, my dear. I positively insist." The secretary laughed lightly. "After all, I spend so much time with your father, I'm practically one of the family."

Christy's eyes darkened speculatively as the door closed behind the secretary, then she tossed a spike of purple hair out of her eyes and grinned cheerfully at her father. "Food!" she exclaimed. "Lead us to the kitchen. It's a major emergency. I have to eat before I pass out."

Christy and her father kept up a nonstop stream of chatter while Laura prepared a simple meal of lasagna and tossed green salad.

"I almost found you once last year," Bennett told his daughter. "My detectives discovered you were at boarding school in England and I flew over right away. The headmistress told me you'd left two days before I arrived, but she had no idea where your mother had taken you."

"We went to Paris," Christy said gloomily. "And then to the Riviera. It was yucky. I knew you must have found me at school. Mom pulled me out of class so fast, I didn't even have time to say good-bye to my friends."

Laura could hear the pain in Christy's voice, and her father obviously heard it too, because he squeezed her hand comfortingly and quickly asked her another question. "You didn't mind going to a boarding school in a foreign country? What was it like?"

"Well, it rained a lot and the uniforms were scratchy, and the food was the pits, but the classes were kind of interesting and the girls were pretty okay. Some of the teachers were even kind of cool. That's where I learned to do my hair and makeup and everything."

"In an English boarding school?" Laura exclaimed, setting the bowl of salad in the center of the table. "You learned to dye your hair purple in an English girls' boarding school?"

"Sure. Lots of the girls there were really into punk fashions, and at weekends we could dress how we liked. The teachers didn't care too much how we did our hair, as long as we finished our homework and won all the lacrosse matches. Most of my friends had pink hair, but our uniforms were green and I thought purple looked better—sort of funky, you know."

"Definitely funky," Laura agreed faintly. Her preconceived notions of life in a British boarding school underwent some rapid revisions, but she still found it difficult to visualize stately oak-beamed corridors filled with hordes of rainbow-haired students. She added a dish of butter and a loaf of heat-and-eat French bread to the food already on the table.

"Here, Christy, this should keep you going until the lasagna is hot."

Christy washed her hands at the kitchen sink, then attacked the food with a gusto that would have worried Laura if she hadn't been accustomed to seeing her teenaged nephews devour their food at a similar speed. Like high-powered bulldozers leveling a building site, she thought with amusement. When she put the bubbling dish of lasagna on the table, Christy's eyes closed in rapt appreciation, and Bennett Logan's laughing gaze suddenly met Laura's over his daughter's head. A flash of genuine, shared amusement shot between them.

"You're obviously a master chef," he said, watching Laura serve generous portions of tender noodles, spicy sauce, and golden melted cheese. "I've never understood how two people can follow identical directions on a package of frozen food and produce two entirely different results. I always seem to end up with a lump that's burned black around the edges and frozen solid in the middle."

"As long as you don't say it must be my woman's touch."

He grinned. "Hey, I'm too smart to go public with a remark like that, even if I think it."

Christy stopped eating just long enough to drink a glass of milk, then she put her glass down and yawned widely. "Oh no!" she exclaimed, her expression tragic. "I haven't got room for a second helping."

"It's probably better if you don't eat too much tonight," her father consoled her. "Why don't we plan on getting up early tomorrow and making a huge stack of pancakes?"

"With sausage?"

"Bacon, too."

"Sounds great to me." She yawned again, then smiled shyly at her father. "All I want to do now is take a boiling hot shower and fall into bed. Isn't it great to think that we have all day tomorrow, just to be together?"

"It's fabulous," he agreed, squeezing her hand very tight. "I'll come and say good night soon, sweetheart. Do you remember where your room is? Upstairs, at the end of the hallway and—"

"And the first door on the right," Christy finished triumphantly. "You see, Dad, I haven't forgotten my last vacation with you! I even remembered that you always come to Denver in May, when the filming for *Empire* is on hiatus." She carried her plates over to the sink, then smiled at Laura, her eyes heavy with sleep now that she . could afford to let her guard down.

"Thank you for helping me find my father. Do you think maybe you could come out with me for a pizza over the weekend? There used to be a great place just around the corner from here."

"I'd like that a lot," Laura said. "But before you go to bed, Christy, I have a question to ask you one last time. How can I contact your mother? You may think that she isn't worried about you, but I think you're wrong, and I have a duty as a police officer to let her know that you're safe. You must tell me how I can reach her, that's the law."

Christy glanced quickly at her father, then looked away again without saying anything. "My mother's in New York," she admitted finally. "She's planning to be there for another week and I know she isn't worrying about me because she thinks I'm staying with friends in Lake Tahoe."

"Then how about your friends? Surely they must be wondering where you are."

"No, because they think I'm in Manhattan with my mother and their cabin doesn't have a phone, so nobody is expecting anybody to call anybody. Honestly, I spent ages planning everything so that nobody would worry, but you can call my mother's house if you like, to confirm that she isn't home. She lives on Sunrise Drive in Greenacres, and the phone number is 555-1212. I think she's staying at the Plaza in New York, but I'm not sure. She didn't tell me exactly where she was going."

Laura wrote down the information without comment. Christy's mother seemed to have been extremely casual in making her child-care arrangements, but it was still good to know that the woman hadn't spent the past week frantically calling home to an empty house and imagining the worst about her daughter.

Laura pocketed her notebook. "Thanks for the address," she said, smiling as she watched Christy's eyes droop shut. "Good night, young lady. You'd better hop into bed before you keel over. I'll try not to keep your father more than a few minutes."

"If he's more than a few minutes, I'll be asleep." Christy hugged her father one last time and trailed out of the room, her entire body drooping with weariness.

Bennett watched his daughter climb the stairs, then he strode back into the kitchen and sat down beside Laura at the wooden table. He took her hand, holding it between both of his, and her heart immediately began its imitation of an out-of-control roller coaster.

"I want to thank you again for bringing Christy home to me," he said softly. "There doesn't seem to be any adequate way to express my gratitude, but if you can think of something, then just tell me what it is."

His smile, Laura decided, was doing irreparable damage to her nervous system. How long could a person's pulse pound in double time before it collapsed from the strain? She removed her hand from his clasp and concentrated on thinking professional police officer–type thoughts, an activity for which her body seemed to have little enthusiasm. Her body, regrettably, was much more interested in considering whether Bennett Logan's broad chest was really as muscular as it looked beneath the thin cotton knit of his shirt. And his mouth . . . How would it feel, she wondered, to let those firm, sensuous lips move urgently against your skin, coaxing your body into a hot, trembling passion? She pulled herself up sharply, shocked by the direction her thoughts had taken. She spoke breezily in an attempt to cover her confusion.

"All I did was take your daughter into protective custody when I saw her running away from a young thug on Colfax Avenue, Mr. Logan. Unfortunately, that's a fairly routine part of my job. In a typical week I pick up at least one runaway. Last week I picked up four, and the youngest was only ten."

He winced. "Do you think Christy was . . . hurt . . . trying to get here?"

"It depends what you mean by hurt. I don't think she was physically assaulted, but no child can hitchhike a thousand miles across country without acquiring some emotional wounds. She'll need to be watched carefully over the next few months."

"How quickly do you think her wounds will heal if she's allowed to settle down into a normal, stable routine?"

She gave him what reassurance she could. "Don't worry too much, Mr. Logan. The kids I've worked with seem to be amazingly resilient once they're convinced that somebody really cares about them. But try to impress upon Christy that running away is a dangerous method of solving her problems. The streets can be cruel teachers."

"She'll have no reason to run away from me," he

replied tersely. He paced the room, his tall, lean body radiating energy. "You said you had a couple of minor problems to clear up with me, Sergeant. Could you explain what they are? Naturally, I'm anxious to go upstairs and say good night to my daughter."

"Of course." Laura gave him a crisp, professional smile, taking care to avoid meeting his eyes. She'd discovered that if she didn't actually look at him, her knees didn't wobble and her heart didn't perform acrobatics, which made it slightly easier to remember that she was a police officer on active duty, not an infatuated female meeting her fantasy lover.

"I won't keep you much longer, Mr. Logan." She winced inwardly as she heard the determined brightness of her tone. "I just need to see your divorce decree, or some other court order that gives you the right to claim joint custody of your daughter with her mother. I'm sure you understand that, as a police officer, I have to be especially careful to avoid violating any court orders concerning Christy's well-being."

Her words fell into a deep pool of silence. "I can't show you a divorce decree or any custody orders," Bennett Logan said finally. "I'm sorry, Sergeant, but I keep all that sort of thing in my lawyer's office."

"It doesn't have to be the original document," she explained quickly. "A photocopy will do just as well."

His expression became sardonic and he suddenly looked very much like Harrison Brand, the black sheep, world-weary millionaire whose character he portrayed on *Empire*. "Sergeant Forbes," he said with exaggerated patience, "my divorce from Renee was finalized four and a half years ago. From that day to this, nobody has ever asked to see a copy of the decree except my lawyer and my accountant, one of whom lives in New York and the other in Los Angeles. I'll call them first thing tomorrow morning and ask them to send me all the relevant documents in the mail. In the meantime, I can't show you any papers concerning Christy's custody arrangements, because I don't have them here in Denver. I only live in this house for about four months of each year, you know."

Laura almost apologized for having bothered him, but she pulled herself up short when she realized what she was about to do. Bennett Logan might have the body of an Olympic athlete and the most stunning eyes since Paul Newman, but he still had to obey the law. She lifted her chin and faced him squarely.

"I'm sorry, Mr. Logan, but if you don't have the necessary papers, then I can't leave Christy here with you. Those are police department regulations, and they're absolutely unbreakable. If you think about it, you'll see that they're good rules, designed to protect children."

His mouth tightened. "Are you seriously suggesting that my daughter would be better off in the police station than she is here in my home?"

"Of course not, but laws are made to protect the general public, and we all have to ob—"

"What are you going to do? Wake up my daughter, haul her out of bed, and drag her off to the police station? And then what happens? Do you tie her up in departmental red tape and ship her off to an emergency shelter for juvenile delinquents? How in the hell is that supposed to help her, or me, or anybody else for that matter?"

He sounded scornful and overbearing, but Laura had enough experience to recognize that his arrogance was simply a defense mechanism. He was worried sick about his daughter and frustrated by his inability to control what happened to her. For the first time Laura looked at Bennett Logan and saw neither a television superstar nor a male sex symbol, but only a desperate and unhappy parent.

"I wasn't planning to take your daughter to the police

station," she explained quickly. "I plan to take her back to my apartment. Don't worry, Mr. Logan, she can spend the night with me. I have the day off tomorrow, so I can stay home with her and you can call me as soon as you've been in touch with your lawyers. If you can get those custody documents to me within twenty-four hours, there's no reason for Christy to be booked into police headquarters."

She saw the sudden slump of his shoulders as relief swept over him, but when he spoke again, his voice remained tense. "I appreciate your offer, Sergeant, but my daughter's probably fast asleep already. Why do we have to wake her? What possible difference can it make whether she spends the night here or at your apartment?"

"Legally, it makes a big difference, Mr. Logan. When she's with me, she's in my custody. If I leave her here with you, I've handed her over to you without the necessary authority. I'm sorry, but there's no way I can leave Christy."

He turned away, balling his fists and jamming his hands into the pockets of his slacks in an obvious effort to contain his anger. To her surprise, when he finally swung around and faced her again, all signs of temper had vanished. His mouth had softened into a charming, rueful half-smile and his deep blue eyes twinkled with a beguiling hint of self-mockery.

If his smile hadn't caused the immediate disintegration of her brain, Laura might have remembered more clearly that this was precisely the look Harrison Brand always utilized five minutes before he suckered some unsuspecting female into his nefarious schemes, and ten minutes before he seduced her into his bed. As it was, Laura's malfunctioning brain cells rang only the faintest of warnings before she gazed deep into Bennett's eyes and dizzily returned his smile.

"Look, Laura—you don't mind if I call you Laura,

do you?—we've neither of us been thinking very clearly." His voice was low and subtly caressing, suggesting a special sort of intimacy between them. "Laura, believe me, I only want what's best for Christy, and I think that's what you want, too."

"Certainly it is, but—"

"No buts," he interjected quickly. "At least not until I've told you my plan. I've just realized that there's a very simple solution to our dilemma. You must spend the night here with me and my daughter. That way, you've never surrendered custody to me, so the law hasn't been broken."

Laura considered his suggestion. "It might be a solution," she admitted cautiously.

"It *is* a solution," he insisted. "Think of the advantages. Christy doesn't have to be woken up, I get to stay with my daughter, the detectives at headquarters don't need to fill out any forms, and you don't break any police department regulations." He grinned with appealing eagerness, looking more like Harrison Brand than ever. "Please say that you'll do it, Laura. Stay here for the night."

His crooked grin would have been irresistible even if her power of rational thought hadn't long since drowned in a flood of hormones. Some instinct did make her hesitate, but what Bennett suggested seemed a reasonable way out of a difficult situation. She was off duty for the next two days, and there was really no compelling reason why she shouldn't stay right here until the missing custody documents arrived from New York, or Los Angeles, or wherever. When all was said and done, she wasn't anxious to uproot Christy again simply for the sake of a mere technicality. However, technicalities could be important in police work, and she needed to be sure that Bennett Logan clearly understood her position.

"If I do agree to stay here, Mr. Logan, you'll be stuck with me for more than a night. I'll have to stay with Christy until a copy of your divorce decree arrives here in Denver."

The faintest of frowns creased his brow, then disappeared almost before she had noticed it. "My friends call me Ben," he said. "I wish you'd call me that, too. And as for staying here tomorrow, it will be a pleasure to have you around, Laura."

He sounded so charmingly sincere that only a tiny part of her mind thought to ask why a major television star would be so pleased at the prospect of spending the day with an off-duty police sergeant. She pushed the question aside, smiling shyly.

"I'm going to need some things from my apartment—"

"No problem, I'll drive you over there myself. Could you wait until tomorrow morning, so that we don't have to disturb Christy? I'm sure we can find a new toothbrush and anything else you might need for tonight. I have a cotton pullover that would probably make a comfortable nightshirt for you."

Laura thought about wearing one of Bennett Logan's shirts and a frisson of pleasure rippled up her spine. Fortunately, her sense of humor came to the rescue before she could revert to total adolescence, and she gave a little chuckle of laughter. Ben raised one eyebrow in silent inquiry, but she shook her head, refusing to explain her amusement. "Let's check on Christy, shall we?" she suggested. "If she's still awake, she'll be wondering what's happened to you."

Christy, however, was deeply asleep. With her makeup washed off, her face looked heartbreakingly vulnerable against the candy-striped pillowcase. Her spiked hair looked pathetic rather than bizarre, somehow emphasizing the youthful fragility of her features and the deep shadows under her eyes. There was a bruise on one of her cheeks that hadn't been visible beneath the layers of makeup, and Ben frowned as he reached out and brushed his fingers lightly over the purple mark. Christy stirred, snuggling against his hand, and his eyes darkened as he stroked her thin shoulders. Watching them both, Laura felt a great sense of relief that she hadn't insisted on dragging Christy down to the bleak surroundings of police headquarters. In this instance, she was confident that she had done the right thing in bending regulations a little bit.

Ben didn't speak when they came out of his daughter's bedroom. He strode down the long, oak-paneled hallway almost as if he had forgotten Laura was following him. He finally paused outside an elegant white-and-gilt door.

"You should be comfortable in here," he said, pushing open the door and switching on an overhead light. "I'll bring you one of my sweat shirts in just a minute, and I think you'll find everything else you need either in the bathroom, or in one of the dresser drawers. The control panel for the television is attached to the headboard, and there's a selection of magazines and mystery novels on the bookshelf." He opened a sliding door on the bottom shelf of the wall unit. "If you'd like a drink, there's sodas and fruit juices in this fridge."

She nodded an acknowledgment, overwhelmed by the luxury of her surroundings. The room was at least as large as her entire apartment, and looked as if it had served as the model for a center spread in *House Beautiful*. Her feet sank inches deep into the carpet as she walked toward the enormous, satin-draped bed.

She turned back the cover and sat down, keeping her knees pressed tightly together. "This looks much too big for one person," she said, then blushed scarlet as she realized just how Ben might interpret her remark.

He didn't make any of the obvious comebacks. Instead, he looked at her in silence for a minute, then turned away with an oddly defensive movement of his shoulders. "Renee has never cared about Christy," he said abruptly. "Will you try to remember that, Laura? And to remember that I love my daughter very much."

Her instincts as a police officer told her that Ben had just said something deeply significant, but for the life of her she couldn't work out what. Before she had time to probe the thought any further, he had crossed the room and seated himself casually on the bed.

He turned to face her, reaching out his hand with the unconscious arrogance of a man whose overtures were never rejected. He crooked his finger beneath her chin and gently tilted her face upward. With the tip of his finger he slowly traced the outline of her lips, then he bent his head and brushed her mouth in a chaste and fleeting kiss.

Neither of them moved after the brief kiss ended. His gaze locked with hers and, for a split second, she thought she saw remorse in his eyes. Then he got up from the bed and walked quickly toward the door.

He paused for a moment in the shadows of the hallway. "Good night, Laura," he said softly. "Sleep well, and thank you again for bringing my daughter home to me."

Chapter Three

LAURA WAS SHOWERED and dressed by seven-thirty the next morning. Despite the early hour, when she went downstairs she discovered Ben and Christy already in the kitchen, eating their way through a stack of butter-drenched blueberry pancakes.

Christy seemed genuinely pleased to see her. She smiled a welcome and scooted her chair around the table, making room for Laura to sit down.

"Hi, did you sleep well? Dad told me you spent the night at our house. Come and eat breakfast. We've made the most awesome pancakes."

Laura walked into the warm kitchen, which smelled of an enticing morning mixture of coffee and bacon. She was glad to see that the shadows were gone from Christy's eyes and that her cheeks had taken on a faint tinge of color. Even Christy's hair looked healthier. She had obviously spent some time in the shower with the shampoo bottle, transforming yesterday's aggressive spikes into a halo of purple fuzz that framed her face with an oddly appealing piquancy.

Ben, dressed in faded chinos and a white cotton-knit shirt, rose politely to his feet as Laura reached the table. For an instant she had the impression that his face was a little taut, his brilliant blue eyes unusually dark; then he smiled and she was conscious of nothing except the urgent need to command her stomach to stop performing flip-flops.

"I hope you slept well," he said, pulling out her chair and offering her the jug of orange juice. He made sure that her plate was filled with pancakes and bacon, then settled back in his seat and took a long sip of coffee. "Christy and I were discussing how we should spend our day," he remarked. "We both decided that you looked as if you were the sort of healthy person who'd enjoy spending the day outdoors, doing something active. Were we right?"

Laura winced. She had spent her entire life being told that she looked healthy and athletic. Most of the men she met considered her a "great guy," and quickly learned to treat her as one of the boys. For years that hadn't bothered her, but recently she'd begun to wish men would notice she had soft, kissable lips and long, fluttery eyelashes as well as a lithe body, firm muscles, and a friendly disposition. She thought wistfully of Ben's current lover on *Empire*—a willowy blonde whose husky voice breathed undiluted sex appeal into the airwaves—and barely repressed a sigh. However, she had learned long ago not to yearn for the unattainable, so she acknowledged Ben's remarks with a cheerful smile.

"You're right, I love spending time outdoors, especially in the mountains. I've done quite a bit of cycling and rock climbing, and I ski during the winter."

"Great!" Christy exclaimed. "What do you think,

Dad? Can we go white-water rafting? It's so much fun when you go over one of the rapids and the rocks are sticking up out of the water and you have to keep paddling because otherwise you think maybe you're gonna drown." She eyed the last bite of pancake on her plate and regretfully decided that she couldn't eat it. "Wouldn't you like to go rafting, Sergeant Forbes?"

"Yes, but unfortunately it's not safe this early in the year, at least for beginners. The spring thaw brings all the snow down from the mountains, so the rivers are too high and too cold for rafting until June. You'll have to wait another couple of weeks, and even then you might need a special wet suit."

At that moment Prudence Datscher came into the kitchen, her brisk footsteps drowning out Christy's groan of protest.

"Good morning, Ben. Good morning, Christy. My word, we're all up bright and early this morning." Prudence poured herself a cup of coffee and gave a little start, as if seeing Laura for the first time.

"Oh, and our police officer is still with us, too. I certainly didn't expect to see you here this morning, Sergeant."

Laura rose to her feet. Even standing up, she realized ruefully, she was a good three inches shorter than Prudence. "Police departments run on red tape, Ms. Datscher," she said pleasantly. "There were a few technicalities to be resolved before I could leave Christy alone with her father."

"I'm sorry to hear that. I hope all the problems have been cleared up now? You must be anxious to get back to your own apartment."

"There are still a couple of minor matters outstanding, Ms. Datscher, but I'm sure they'll soon be taken care of."

Prudence clamped her lips together, then smiled carefully. "Well, it's certainly good to know we have one of

Denver's finest hard at work on our behalf. Don't let me disturb your breakfast, Sergeant."

She opened the folder she was carrying and turned toward her employer. "Ben, I'm sorry to intrude on your get-together with your daughter, but we do have a busy schedule today. Ronnie needs your response to that script he sent, and at ten we scheduled an interview with the 'Lifestyle' reporter from the *Tribune*. You're eating lunch with Cheston Berkowitz and then at two o'clock we—"

"Hey, slow down for a moment, Pru." Ben raised his hand in mock protest as he took the sheaf of papers his secretary held out to him. He flicked over the typed pages, rumpling Christy's hair absentmindedly as he read.

"You're right, this is all important stuff, but today is a special occasion and work will have to wait. Tell Ronnie I'll read his script tonight without fail and get back to him before breakfast tomorrow. Apologize to Cheston Berkowitz and ask him if he'd be prepared to reschedule for early next week. As for the rest, Pru, I'll rely on you to keep the wolves at bay. Explain that I'm dealing with some urgent personal business, but don't specify what."

"Do you think it's wise to cancel out on the *Tribune* reporter at the last minute? She has a reputation for being venomous when she's thwarted. There was that article she did on Michael—"

"I think it's essential," he interrupted gently. "My daughter and I haven't seen each other for four years and we have some catching up to do. Besides, the studio seems to have forgotten that I'm supposed to be on vacation. They scheduled all those interviews and luncheons, not me."

"Yes, of course, Ben, I understand. Don't worry, I'll make your excuses."

"Good." He grinned engagingly. "Tell everybody I'll fit them in before I go back to California, without fail.

And, Prudence, I'm relying on you to be your usual efficient, discreet self. I don't want *anybody* to know that Christy's staying with me. We don't want the press hounds scenting this story."

Laura had busied herself stacking breakfast dishes in the sink, but she turned around just in time to spot a look of mutual understanding flash between Ben and his secretary. Prudence's reply, however, gave no clue as to what silent agreement they had reached. "I'd better get busy canceling some of these appointments," the secretary said, and walked quickly from the room.

Faintly uneasy, Laura dried her hands on a paper towel. "Ben, those documents we spoke about last night," she interjected. "Have you managed to get in touch with your lawyer about them?"

"Sure have," he responded easily. "I called Aaron's home first thing this morning. Because of the time difference it was already eight o'clock in New York, but I managed to catch him before he left for the office. He promised me Federal Express would have the papers by ten o'clock, East Coast time. Don't worry, Laura, you'll have everything the police department needs in your hands well before noon tomorrow."

"What papers are you talking about?" Christy asked.

Ben returned the pitcher of orange juice to the fridge. "Just boring legal stuff," he said casually. "Don't worry your head about it, honeybun. What we need to decide right now is where we're going to spend the rest of the day. That Colorado sunshine's too wonderful to waste sitting indoors talking."

Laura's little niggle of uneasiness faded away, so that she wasn't even quite sure what it was that had bothered her. "We could drive to Minturn and hike up one of the easy mountain trails," she suggested. "I've climbed the Mount of the Holy Cross a couple of times already, and there's one trail that's safe even for inexperienced climbers. We wouldn't need any special equipment except sturdy walking shoes."

"We can just walk up it?" Christy wrinkled her nose, as if to suggest that any mountain that didn't require pitons, ropes, and an ax or two was hardly worth tackling. But when it became apparent that her climbing experience was limited to watching other people perform on television, Ben overruled her pleas that they should attempt something more exciting.

"You might take a camera if your father has one," Laura recommended. "We should see some interesting wildlife. Deer for sure, and maybe a bighorn sheep and a marmot or two if we're lucky."

The hope of spotting some deer, perhaps with their fawns, was enough to reconcile Christy to the prospect of climbing a mountain that didn't require much skill other than an abundant supply of energy and a pair of strong sneakers. She ran upstairs quite happily to pick up a sweater and the waterproof nylon jacket that she had brought with her from California.

Laura needed to go home so that she could change, and the three of them arrived at her apartment less than forty minutes later. She parked her Ford in its assigned spot, then took Christy upstairs with her while Ben opted to drive around the block. "I don't want to get another parking ticket," he said. "Those darn Denver police seem to have a grudge against me and my poor old Mercedes. Every time I leave it anywhere, we get a ticket."

Laura grinned. "I'm not rising to the bait, Ben. After five years as a cop, I've learned to run for cover when people start talking about their parking problems. Come on, Christy, let's hurry."

They stopped in the lobby to check Laura's mailbox, and she found a letter from David, her eldest brother, wedged between her telephone bill and a pile of circulars. She scooped up the mail with trembling fingers and hurried upstairs to her second-floor apartment. She settled Christy in the living room with an illustrated book on Colorado wildlife, then hurried into her bedroom, kicking the door closed. Her hands were damp with sweat as she ripped open the envelope containing her brother's letter.

As she had feared, David's news was all bad, despite his determined effort to gloss over the worst of it. The local bank, financially strapped by the sheer volume of its outstanding farm loans, was going to foreclose on her family's property in Iowa. By the end of the summer, when the crops were in, the land that had first been tilled a hundred years ago by her great-grandfather would be put up for public auction. After four successful generations, the Forbes family would no longer be Iowa farmers. Tears blurred her eyes as she read her brother's final paragraph.

Don't you worry about things, Laura. You've done everything you could to help, and we're mighty grateful, but I guess we're all having to learn the tough lesson that sometimes our best just isn't good enough. Anne and our boys are fine, likewise Jim and all of his family. Mother is taking this real hard, as you'd expect, but she lived through the tail end of the Depression and she understands that sometimes backbreaking work isn't enough to prevent disaster. In fact, Jim and I are luckier than some of the folks around here. We've both been offered the chance of work in town at the hardware store, so at least we won't have to go on welfare. I don't think Jim or I would have handled that real well.

Laura crumpled the letter into a ball and tossed it onto her bed, reaching blindly for the buttons on her uniform blouse as she started to undress. It wasn't fair, she thought helplessly. Dammit, it just wasn't right that international politics and wild price fluctuations could force a prosperous family business into bankruptcy, particularly since even the bank agreed that the Forbes farm was run with exceptional efficiency. If only her brothers had the cash to pay off some of their outstanding debts, she knew that the farm could be operated profitably in the long run, perhaps even in the fairly near future. She fumbled in the closet for her jeans, fighting back tears. Her brothers might need *only* a few thousand dollars of ready cash, but she had no way of raising it and neither did they.

She picked up the letter, smoothing it out and rereading the final page. She wasn't deceived by David's attempt at cheerfulness. She knew all too well what sort of money he and their brother Jim would earn doing odd jobs at a hardware store in a depressed agricultural town. If her sisters-in-law and two older nephews managed to find jobs—a very big *if* in rural Iowa—her family might be able to afford adequate food and cheap housing, but it was going to be close. And what in the world would their mother do? Laura wondered. Barbara Forbes was a widow whose entire life centered on the farm. For nearly forty years her days had been filled with baking, cleaning, sewing, and turning the abundant produce of the farm into jellies, jams, preserves, and pickles that were the envy of the local community. How would such a woman fill her days in a tiny apartment in the center of town? To Laura's mother, a town of fifteen hundred people would seem as noisy and confining as downtown Manhattan.

Laura put a thick wool sweater into her small nylon backpack and blinked away the last few stubborn tears. In truth, her family's situation was so grim that she could do nothing to alleviate it. Her salary as a police sergeant was generous for one person but totally inadequate for paying off a seventy-thousand-dollar farm loan. Difficult as it was to accept, her family's situation had reached the point where the most she could do was plan to send them lavish gifts at birthdays and Christmas. The ultimate cop-out of a rich relative, she thought with a twinge of bitterness.

She tossed a change of clothing and some makeup into an overnight bag, carrying it and her backpack into the living room. She forced herself to concentrate on Christy's breezy chatter as they made their way downstairs. To her relief, she was able to smile almost naturally when Ben drew up alongside the curb and told them both to hop in. She took one of the back seats, leaving Christy to sit beside her father. At this moment she wasn't sure that she was capable of joining in their lighthearted banter.

The dreary fringe developments of the city were soon left behind as Ben turned onto Interstate 70 with its breathtaking views of the Rocky Mountains. Laura looked at the sun glinting off a distant, snow-covered peak, and her spirits began to lift.

"Oh, neat!" Christy exclaimed, gazing appreciatively at the green slopes of the foothills. "I forgot how terrific the mountains look. Are we nearly there?"

They had been driving for all of twenty minutes and Ben turned around, his eyes meeting Laura's in a silent, wry smile. " 'Fraid not, sweetheart. We have almost another two hours to go."

Christy wriggled despairingly. "Two hours! How can it possibly take so long?"

"Because we have nearly a hundred miles of mountain roads still to cover, and with a cop in the car I have no intention of speeding. Try admiring the wonders of the scenery for a while. See all those trees over on that hill? They're blue spruce, which is the Colorado state tree, and we'll soon be coming up to the old mining town of Idaho Springs."

"What did they mine there?"

"Mostly gold," Laura replied. "There's a five-mile tunnel running underground between here and Central City. It's the longest mining tunnel in the world."

"Can you still find gold there?"

"Tiny pieces. Not enough to make anybody rich."

"Forty thousand gold prospectors traveled through this area in the three years between 1859 and 1861," Ben remarked, surprising Laura by his knowledge of the region's history. "Before that, the Indians had the place pretty much to themselves, except for a few fur traders and the Spanish colonies down in the south."

"Where do the Indians live now?" Christy asked. "On reservations?"

"Some. But most of the Utes were pushed out of Colorado, and a lot of the Arapaho and Comanche were slaughtered by volunteer soldiers who didn't approve of their heathen lifestyle."

"Not to mention their unfortunate habit of removing the settlers' scalps," Laura interjected dryly.

Ben grinned. "That, too. Although even if the Indians didn't launch an attack, the white people usually managed to convince themselves they had good moral reasons for killing them off, especially when it looked like they might interfere with the settlers' profits."

Christy frowned. "You mean the miners didn't really care if the Indians were heathen? They just wanted to take all the gold for themselves?"

"Something like that, although, of course, there were always a few whites around who genuinely wanted to do what was right and best for the Indians."

"That's kind of interesting," Christy remarked, craning her neck for a last look at the huge wooden water wheel that had once controlled the mine sluices at Idaho Springs. "You know, I like hearing about history and stuff except when we have to do it at school."

"Even schools sometimes manage to make history interesting," Ben said. "I'm sure we'll manage to find at least one good history teacher when we register you for junior high tomorrow."

"Tomorrow! Oh, Dad, I don't need to start school here! It's so close to summer vacation that it's hardly worth you doing all that boring paperwork."

"It's no trouble," he said quietly. "When were you last registered for school, Christy?"

She looked away. "I was in school until December," she said, with a touch of defiance. "You know, like I told you. In England."

Ben greeted her statement in silence and she burst out, "It's not my fault! Mom never wanted me to go to school in California! She was planning to move to New York with Eric and she said there was no point in having me start school in Greenacres when I'd only have to leave a few weeks after she went to all the trouble of getting me enrolled."

Whatever he may have thought about his ex-wife's neglectful attitude, Ben made no attempt to criticize her behavior, or even to reproach Christy. He obviously realized that few thirteen-year-olds possessed the self-discipline to put themselves into school when their mother was tacitly encouraging them to play hooky.

"That's all in the past, Christy," he said evenly. "We need to concentrate on planning for the future. Luckily you're very bright, so if you work hard over the summer, you might be allowed to enroll in ninth grade next fall. If not, it won't be the end of the world. You're young for your grade level, so it won't matter too much if you have to repeat the final year of junior high."

Christy pouted rebelliously. "I don't want to repeat eighth grade. Repeating is for dummies."

Ben ignored her deliberate provocation. "In your case, you've missed so much it would hardly be repeating, would it? But don't worry, honey. Before the summer's through, I'm sure you'll be able to convince the school administration you're not a dummy—even though you goofed off for five months."

Christy's cheeks flamed scarlet and Laura took pity on the child's evident embarrassment, although she agreed completely with Ben's insistence that his daughter enroll in summer school. "Look!" she exclaimed. "There are five mule deer over there on the trail. Can you see them? They don't usually venture this close to the highway."

Everybody's attention was successfully diverted, and for the remainder of the drive even Christy was so impressed by the grandeur of the Rockies that she forgot to protest she was bored.

They reached Vail and turned off the highway into the White River National Forest. After negotiating a series of hair-raising switchbacks on the dirt road that led to Notch Mountain Creek, they parked the car and set out on the hiking trail that wound up the mountain toward Half Moon Pass.

The curving summit of the Mount of the Holy Cross, named for the two giant, snow-filled fissures on its northeastern face, thrust into the cloudless blue sky with stark, picture-postcard perfection. Although it was only May, the sun was hot on their backs as they walked, and Laura felt a familiar rush of anticipation as she gazed up at the granite peak and imagined clambering out onto the topmost ledge, fourteen thousand feet above sea level.

She soon realized that they weren't likely to reach the summit that day. Ben was in superb physical condition and he obviously had lots of experience as a rock climber. But Christy, accustomed to living at sea level, was bothered by the thin oxygen of the higher altitude, and never quite managed to catch her stride, despite lots of unobtrusive help from both her father and Laura.

After an hour and a half of hiking they were still below the timberline, but the trail had broadened into a natural resting place. Ben looked sympathetically at his daughter, who was huffing and puffing with the effort of taking each new step. "Want to stop for a few minutes?" he asked, slipping his backpack from his shoulders and pretending a fatigue Laura was sure he wasn't feeling.

Christy came to an immediate halt. "I sure do! Boy, I thought you two were going to keep going for*ever!*" Without waiting for any further encouragement, she stretched out on a nearby boulder, groaning loudly as her aching muscles adjusted themselves to the contours of the rock. "I'm dead," she announced to the world. "Totally dead."

"You'd better put some more sunblock on your nose," Laura said, holding out a tube she had taken from her backpack. "You don't want to be sunburned as well as dead."

Christy opened one eye. "The sun isn't all that hot."

"But at this altitude it's easy to burn even when it feels cold."

Still lying down, Christy applied sunscreen to her face. Ben held up two plastic bottles he'd taken from his backpack. "You two want some water?" he asked.

"Sounds wonderful." Laura spotted another boulder only a few feet from Christy's, and sighed with pleasure as she sat down on a patch of spiky sedge grass. She propped herself against the smooth, sun-warmed rock and closed her eyes, lifting her face to the sky and pushing a curl of slightly damp hair away from her neck. Through the rustle of the leaves, she heard the nervous squeak of a coney and, somewhere in the distance, the distinctive flapping of a blue grouse's wings as it prepared for takeoff.

Christy yawned noisily. "How high up have we climbed?"

"We're almost twelve thousand feet above sea level. Just a hundred feet to go before we reach the tree line."

"Another hundred feet!" Christy exclaimed darkly.

"Good grief, Dad! Just remember I'm already a walking corpse. I can't think where people as old as you two get all your energy."

"We work at it," Ben said, exchanging a rueful grin with Laura. "But at our age, it's a painful struggle. Right, Laura?"

"Right." She smiled at him in shared amusement. "In fact, you'd better fetch that water, Ben, before your decrepit old bones give out on you."

She watched as he strode across the trail, expertly negotiating the slippery stones and gravel surrounding a narrow waterfall of cascading, freshly melted snow. Sweat beaded his forehead and he dashed it off impatiently with the sleeve off his sweater, then set the bottles on the ground, splashing the icy, foaming water onto his face.

Last night he had kissed her. The thought flashed into Laura's mind, seemingly out of nowhere. If he kissed her again, right now, his skin would feel cool against her hot cheeks and his mouth would taste of crystal-clear mountain water. A spark of sexual awareness flared deep inside her, making her heart pound, and she clamped her arms tightly around her waist, irritated by the reactions of her own body.

Yesterday evening, when she first met Ben, there had been some excuse for her juvenile response to his sexual magnetism. He was, after all, an actor whose television role as Harrison Brand had been carefully developed to arouse feminine fantasies. And, dammit, Laura was very much a woman, despite the determination of her colleagues to treat her as one of the boys. But today, after several hours in Ben's company, she surely ought to be able to distinguish between Harrison Brand, the sex symbol, and Ben Logan, the father in a disputed custody case. However much she enjoyed his company, she couldn't afford to forget that she was a police officer—and that Ben was the father of a runaway she had taken into protective custody.

He came back with two brimming water bottles and gave one to Christy, along with a chocolate-coated granola bar. Then he walked over to Laura's side and handed her the other bottle.

"Could I please share your rock?" he asked, smiling. "Christy has spreadeagled herself across most of the other one."

"Be my guest." Laura took a long sip of the ice-cold water and eased to one side of the grass patch as Ben sat down. He reached for his backpack and retrieved two more granola bars before offering one to Laura. They munched in companionable silence, the heat of the early afternoon sun just sufficient to counteract the springtime chill in the wind.

"It's beautiful up here today," Ben said, leaning his head against the boulder. "I'm really glad we came."

"I like the mountains better at this time of year than in the winter," Laura agreed.

"Even though you're a skier?"

"Mmm, yes. When you climb a mountain, you feel more intimately connected to it than if you're just skimming over the surface on a pile of packed snow. I climbed the east face of Longs Peak last August, and by the time I reached the top, that mountain was *mine.*"

"The east face is quite a climb," Ben said, and Laura was ridiculously pleased by the admiration in his voice. "Have you ever tried Sharkstooth? My mountaineering friends tell me it's a real killer."

"No, but it's on my list for the end of the summer, when I've had a chance to get in better shape."

"I'd say you're in pretty spectacular shape already," Ben commented lazily. Through half-closed eyes he watched the progress of a solitary cloud scudding across the sky, his shoulder pressed companionably against her. "Sometimes, when I get this high up on a mountain, I wonder why in the world I bother to go back down again."

"I don't think you'd make a very convincing mountain hermit," Laura said dryly. "Besides, you need an audience for your talent. Playing to the chipmunks would get tedious after a while."

He gave her the barest hint of a smile, sitting up to take the water bottle from her and swallowing a generous swig. "An audience for my talent, huh? That's a kind way of expressing it. In my darker moments I suspect that what I really need is a fan club for my oversized ego."

She shrugged. "Maybe you do, but is that so bad? After all, public approval's an important part of acting. Surely most actors draw strength from the admiration of their audience."

Ben's startlingly blue eyes focused on her with new intensity. "That's an interesting thought. Is your family connected with the theater, Laura?"

She pulled up a blade of grass and chewed on the sweet white tip to conceal the immediate ache that mention of her family caused. "Not at all. They're farmers, born and bred in Iowa. The only time my parents ever went to the theater was in New York on their honeymoon. They went to Radio City Music Hall, and my mother can still give you a blow-by-blow account of the entire program."

"You're from Iowa? How come a nice Iowa farm girl ended up chasing criminals in the big city?"

"That's easy to explain," she said wryly. "The nice Iowa farm boy I was engaged to eloped with my college roommate two days before our wedding. I came to Denver to drown my sorrows."

"And did you succeed?"

"Oh, yes. For the first two weeks I was suicidally depressed. For the next two months I went through my world-weary and cynical state—all men are beasts and betrayers, you know the kind of stuff. Since then, I've been thanking God on a daily basis that Russ had more sense than I did. We'd have been miserably unhappy together. I realize now that I wasn't cut out to be a farmer's wife."

"You don't exactly look cut out to be a sergeant on the Denver police force, either. You don't seem to have enough hard edges. Do you like your job?"

"*Like* is maybe the wrong word. My work's usually interesting and occasionally rewarding. On the other hand, it's sometimes the pits. There are nights when you wonder where all the decent human beings are hiding themselves."

"That must be when you think about the farm in Iowa," he said quietly. "You remember the smell of the earth after a spring rain, or the sun shining down on a field bursting with ripe corn, and then the world seems an okay place again."

"I guess that's pretty much what I do." But not for long, she thought. Soon the farm would belong to an investment corporation, and her memories would lose their reality. The corporation would, no doubt, tear down the sprawling farmhouse with its huge kitchen, odd-shaped living room, and cosy but inefficient bedrooms. Her mother's vegetable garden would disappear, along with the chicken coop, and the swing hanging from a cross beam in the barn.

The prospect was too painful to contemplate and she jumped up quickly, brushing a few granola crumbs from her sweater. "Do you know, it's one-thirty already. Unless we hurry, we're not going to make it to the timberline before we have to turn around and start the climb down." She raised her voice a little. "Hey, Christy, how are you doing over there? Still dead?"

The chocolate bar seemed to have given Christy a second wind. "I'm terrific," she said, springing up with alacrity and humming a marching song as she stepped out onto the trail. She froze suddenly in her tracks, pointing to the sparse underbrush up ahead. "What is it?" she asked. "The little animal at the edge of the trail?"

"It's a marmot," Laura said softly.

"A yellow-bellied marmot," Ben amplified. "Try to take a picture before it runs away."

Christy snapped two or three shots in quick succession, then the dumpy little animal scurried across the dirt path and hid beneath a small overhanging rock. Convinced that she would be able to track the marmot silently enough to get a close-up shot, Christy crept along the trail, first whispering to Ben and Laura that they should stay put so as not to add to the noise.

"I'm going to rinse the chocolate off my fingers," Laura said, walking over to the waterfall and holding her hands under the glistening spray. "How about you?"

"Good idea." Ben joined her, leaning back against a shelf of dry rock and watching the sunlight refract through the foam into a dancing rainbow of color. The noise of the tumbling water drowned out all other sounds and the angle of the waterfall hid them from the trail. A gust of wind skimmed across Laura's cheek, blowing tendrils of hair into her face, but she didn't reach up and push the offending curls out of her eyes, as she would normally have done. Instead, she looked up at Ben and felt warmth suffuse her cheeks.

For a long time he returned her gaze in silence, then he reached out and touched her face, looping the soft strands of hair behind her ears. Slowly he traced the line of her cheeks with a fingertip, and she closed her eyes, not wanting him to see how deeply his touch affected her. For a moment he seemed to hesitate, then he brushed his thumb across her lips, tilting her chin gently upward.

She pushed her palms flat against the rock behind her. He was going to kiss her, and she wasn't prepared for it. She was too inexperienced, too dangerously attracted, too—

His mouth descended on hers, light and cool and frighteningly experienced. Laura trembled as the kiss deepened, her palms pressing into the rock until they hurt. Kissing Bennett Logan was highly hazardous to her mental health, and if she had a grain of sense, she would walk away before her star-struck infatuation toppled over into something infinitely more dangerous.

But she didn't move, and Ben's arms went around her waist, pulling her hard against his body. Her hands lost their grip on the jagged rock and crept up to cling around his neck.

"You taste of mountains," he murmured against her mouth. "Mountains and cold spring water."

The sudden, sharp heat in the pit of her stomach was unnerving. The pressure of his mouth against hers was no longer enjoyable or even exciting, but painfully urgent—a burning necessity that demanded her response. Her lips parted, welcoming the fierce thrust of his tongue. She could feel her body melting into soft curves that molded around his hardness. She could feel the coolness of his lips warming into passion. It was torture. And she wanted it to last forever.

Chapter Four

SHE TASTED HOT and sweet and altogether too damn *real*. Ben wasn't prepared for it and he sure as hell didn't like it. He couldn't understand why he was feeling this totally unwelcome flare of genuine passion. Dammit, he hadn't intended anything more than a casual kiss, an offhand sort of thank you for a pleasant day.

Like hell that was all you intended, some aggravating shred of conscience rebuked him. Face it, fella, you knew good and well Laura wasn't used to playing in your sort of league. You *wanted* to throw her off-balance. You hoped one of your expert, packaged-for-television kisses would keep her simmering in a convenient state of star-struck blindness.

He was already tense with desire when her hips moved forward, thrusting innocently against his body. He was sure she had no conscious realization of what she was doing to him. Maybe that was why he found her movements so frustratingly erotic. How long had it been since he wanted a woman this badly? A long time. A dangerously long time.

Deliberately he forced himself to draw back, to shut down his emotions. He imagined a camera poised over his left shoulder, imagined the director requesting a repositioning of his hands. They'd make a lousy shot right at the moment, he thought humorlessly. Both of them were a damned sight too hot and bothered to be photogenic. On camera, glycerine and water always looked a hell of a lot better than genuine sweat.

Ben stepped back, satisfied that his control was once again in place. "We'd better find out what's happened to Christy and her marmot," he said, avoiding Laura's eyes. He was afraid she might look vulnerable, and he didn't want any more burdens added to his overloaded conscience.

"Oh, gosh, I forgot about Christy."

It had to be ten years since he'd last heard an adult woman say *gosh*. Her voice sounded husky, breathless, and a little shy. He couldn't even remember when he'd last met a woman who felt shy after a simple kiss. Most of the women he encountered nowadays wouldn't have raised a blush after participating in a full-fledged technicolor orgy.

Impatient with her, or perhaps with himself, he held out his hand to help her across the slippery stones at the edge of the waterfall, giving her one of his best—and least sincere—smiles. His experience with the long chain of women who'd decorated his life since his divorce had taught him that a charming smile was a terrific way to avoid difficult conversations.

Christy was hurtling down the path toward them and his heart squeezed tight with love at the sight of her. Surely his deception was justified, Ben thought. The law had made a mistake, and anybody who knew the facts would agree that his daughter needed to be kept safe from Renee's vicious maneuverings.

"Guess what!" Christy exclaimed triumphantly. "I took a whole reel of film and I saw a huge bunch of those red flowers you told me about, Dad. The special ones that only grow near the top of a mountain."

"King's crowns," Ben replied absently. Christy's face was flushed with excitement and her eyes gleamed with laughter, the wariness of the day before totally vanquished from her expression.

If only his daughter could have been returned to him by some stolid, coldhearted bureaucrat, then he wouldn't have felt nearly so bad about lying. Laura, unfortunately, was anything but coldhearted, and she didn't deserve to be tricked. A Denver police sergeant obviously couldn't be considered naive, but somehow Laura had managed to retain some of the essential innocence of her country background. He felt like a total heel in deceiving her. He *was* a total heel.

"I think it's time to start the hike back down the mountain," Laura said. "Don't you agree, Ben?"

He looked at her for the first time since breaking off their kiss. Her soft brown eyes were warm and diffident and every bit as vulnerable as he'd feared. Just for once, he decided, he was going to behave semihonorably. However convenient it might be to adopt his Harrison Brand role and seduce Laura into a state of mindless compliance, he wouldn't even try to do it.

He glanced up at the clouds starting to gather in the far west of the sky. "Yes, we'd better turn around right now," he said, making sure his voice sounded polite but impersonal. "We want to be back at the trailhead long before those clouds decide to start dumping on us."

Christy, inevitably, wanted to go on until they reached the summit, but Laura, without any sign of losing her patience, persuaded her that such a climb would be dangerous without special protective weather gear.

Ben strode out on the path, wishing he was tackling something more challenging than an easy scramble down a well-marked hiking trail. Recently he had learned to enjoy climbing some of Colorado's more hazardous peaks. One of the very best things about hanging from a sheer mountain face attached only to a thin rope and a shard of rock was that it didn't leave much time for idle contemplation. Sometimes it was wonderful to have no time to think. Right at the moment, for instance, when he didn't like himself very much.

For the past four years he had believed that if Christy could be returned to him, nothing else would matter. Now he found he didn't want Laura to suffer because of her role in their reunion. Ben decided that he'd check with his lawyers when Renee brought the inevitable court case against him, and see if there was any way to keep Laura's name out of the proceedings. Hell, he paid his lawyers enough that they ought to be able to get Jack the Ripper a reduced sentence for murder, let alone find some way to keep one kindhearted police sergeant out of trouble with her superiors.

It was four o'clock by the time they reached the campground where they had parked the car, and close to five by the time they approached the resort town of Vail on their way back to Denver. By this time Christy was starving, and declared there was no chance of surviving the journey home unless she received an immediate infusion of food.

"How about you, Laura?" Ben asked. "Are you hungry? There are plenty of good restaurants and coffee shops in Vail, if you'd like to stop."

As it happened, she wasn't particularly hungry. Despite her best efforts not to think about Ben's kiss by the waterfall and his studiously polite manner ever since, Laura's stomach was churning too much for food to seem appealing. However, the gaze Christy turned on her was beseeching.

"Sergeant Forbes, *please* say you want to stop! Do

you realize we haven't eaten for nine whole hours? I think that's probably illegal."

Laura forced a smile. "Inhumane, at the very least. I guess a hamburger and a soda does sound pretty good. By the way, I wish you'd call me *Laura*. Sergeant Forbes sounds much too official for two people who just climbed a mountain together."

"Hooray!" Christy gave a giant sigh of relief. "Food and a new friend—this is a great moment. Turn off here, Dad. The sign says this is the exit for the center of town."

They left the Mercedes in a large parking lot and walked over the covered wooden bridge toward the picturesque main street. The cobblestone sidewalks were unexpectedly crowded, and Ben halted warily when he spotted a jostling throng of people and the paneled trucks of three television minicam units all converged on the same small plaza.

"Maybe they've come to do an interview with you, Dad." Christy was only half teasing, and would obviously have been thrilled to watch her father being filmed for the nightly news. *"Famous TV star reunited with long-lost daughter.* How does that sound as a headline?"

Ben winced. "Corny," he said briefly. "Laura, would you mind if we got out of here? With this many people milling around, it would probably be quicker to stop in the next town for Christy's hamburger."

"Fine by me." But Laura managed no more than a couple of steps backward before their return down the narrow street was blocked by a swarm of new arrivals. "We seem to be stuck," she said apologetically. "It's wall-to-wall people in all directions."

"Let's try anyway. I really want to get out of here without being recognized."

Ben sounded grim, even a little nervous. But that was ridiculous, Laura thought. He'd appeared on television regularly for at least ten years, and by now he must be accustomed to dealing with overenthusiastic fans. However, she sympathized with his desire to retain his privacy, and she tapped the shoulder of the man in front of her. "Excuse me, please, we need to get back to the parking lot."

"Honey, I haven't got room to move a finger. What's going on up there, anyways?"

"I've no idea. I can see the mikes and the TV cameras but not who's talking."

"Tell me the worst, Laura." Ben's voice sounded low and husky in her ear. "Do Denver police sergeants arrest men who clear an escape path with their elbows?"

"Only if they jab little old ladies in the stomach."

"Then here goes," he said, shouldering his way in front of his daughter.

"No, wait! We have to find out what's happening." Christy twisted away from her father and darted toward the front of the crowd before either Laura or Ben could grab her. "Pardon me," they heard her say to the woman who finally blocked her path. "But could you tell me what's going on? Why have all these TV people come out to Vail?"

The woman blinked when she saw Christy's purple hair, but she answered in a friendly enough fashion. "It's the vice president of the United States," she explained. "He's in Vail to play a charity golf tournament, and he decided to walk through town to do a little politicking. Of course, all of the local television stations want to interview him. He's explaining the president's views on the crisis in Central America." She broke off irritably to acknowledge the teenager tugging at her sleeve. "What is it, Erin? How many times have I told you not to interrupt when I'm talking to somebody?"

The young girl stood on tiptoe to whisper something in her mother's ear. The woman's eyes suddenly opened wide and she stared past Christy, her gaze fixing avidly on Ben.

"Oh, my heavens, Erin, you're right! It really is! It's him!"

Ben and Laura had finally managed to struggle through the crowd to Christy's side, and the woman seized Ben's hand, pumping it wildly. "My daughter said you were Harrison Brand and so you are. I mean you're Bennett Logan, not Harrison Brand. Of course I know Harrison is just a character on TV. I'm one of your biggest fans, Harris—I mean, Mr. Logan. I've watched every single episode of *Empire* since it first came on, and I think you're wonderful." She poked the ribs of a short, rather plump man standing in front of her. "Frank, turn around for heaven's sake, you'll never guess who's here. It's Harrison Brand from *Empire*. Give me your pen, quick, so I can get his autograph."

By the time Ben wrote the requested message and signed his name in her pocket diary, the vice president had finished his speech. The crowd clapped politely as he was surrounded by a circle of waiting secret service guards and swept into a restaurant commandeered by his entourage. Two of the three television newscasters followed the vice president into the restaurant and the door closed firmly behind them.

But the crowd didn't disperse. News of Bennett Logan's presence rippled through the plaza with the speed of a tidal wave crashing toward shore, and the crowd turned with pleasure to greet a favorite superstar —who, fortunately, seemed likely to know no more than they did about boring subjects like Contras, Costa Ricans, and other bewildering Central American issues.

Ben signed the last piece of paper thrust under his nose and returned it to its owner with a smile and a murmured word of thanks for her compliments. He looked totally at ease, Laura thought, and yet some instinct—or maybe some professional skill derived from her years of interviewing suspects—made her certain that he was hating every moment of what he was doing.

A tiny gap in the crowd opened up to their right and he spotted it at once. He reached out and grabbed Laura's and Christy's hands, shoving them toward the edge of the crowd even as he continued to exchange a few friendly words with his fans.

The apparent escape route turned out to be illusion. The sea of people parted obligingly, but at the end of the passageway Ben found himself face-to-face with a television news camera and a determined reporter.

Laura could feel the sudden increase in tension in his already taut body, and she waited for the explosion. It never came. With an effort of will that she thought nobody else recognized, Ben greeted the reporter with a charming, intimate smile. Simultaneously he moved in front of Christy, shielding her from the reporter's inquisitive gaze.

"Hi, Tessa, how are you doing? You're looking wonderful." He shook the reporter's hand warmly, leaning forward to kiss her lightly on the cheek. "It's been a while."

"Too long, Ben."

"You're right." He glanced back at the throng of people being held in check by the television crew and his smile became rueful. "I suppose there's no hope of appealing to your better nature and asking you to get me out of here? For old times' sake?"

"Sure," she said, a touch of amusement lightening her determined expression. "I'll hide you in the private dining room we've hired—as soon as you've given me a ten-minute exclusive."

He gave a mock sigh. "Did our government ever consider sending you over to make an arms deal with the Russians?"

"No, but maybe I should volunteer my services. Are you going to give me an interview, Ben?"

"Your granite heart is showing, Tess."

She smiled. "How about my shark's teeth? Are they still in place?"

"Every last one of 'em. Unfortunately."

She laughed, sounding almost pleased by the compliment. "Your choice, Ben. My private dining room in exchange for ten minutes of your time, or I tell the boys to let the crowd loose."

The reporter sounded superficially good-humored, but Laura had no doubt that she meant exactly what she said, so she wasn't surprised when Ben shrugged resignedly. "Ten minutes, Tess. I'm timing you."

The reporter signaled immediately to the technicians and positioned herself so that they would need a minimum amount of adjustment to the portable lights. Ben stood at her side, joking quietly with the cameramen but not even glancing toward Laura and his daughter. Laura wondered why he didn't introduce Christy to the newscaster, then realized he probably wanted to protect her from the glare of unwelcome publicity. With the threat of kidnapping and extortion constantly looming over them, celebrities nowadays couldn't afford to expose their families to the limelight. They were both standing very close to Ben, but Laura kept a firm grip on Christy's arm, so that she couldn't suddenly take it into her head to go bouncing on camera. As a police officer, she heartily approved of Ben's caution.

The technicians were finally satisfied that the equipment was functioning properly, and Tessa launched into her opening announcements. "This is Tessa Renier, at Lionshead in Vail. It's an unexpected pleasure for all of us on the Channel Eight News Team to have Bennett Logan with us this afternoon. So tell me, Ben, what are you doing here in Colorado?"

"Taking a short vacation," he replied easily. "Hiking up a few mountains, seeing some old friends, and reading one or two best-sellers."

"I'm sure everybody agrees you've earned some relaxation. You must be delighted that *Empire* has recaptured its position as the season's number one television show. Do you think your torrid on-screen romance with Sapphire, played by Jill Cassell, has anything to do with the show's soaring ratings?"

"The producers seem to think so, and I certainly like working with Jill. She's a talented, hard-working actress and there's a definite chemistry between us when we play a scene together."

"We heard that Harrison Brand's on-screen affair with Sapphire is tame in comparison to the heat being generated by your real-life romance with Ms. Cassell. Is she by any chance sharing your vacation here in the Rocky Mountains?"

Ben's mouth tightened briefly, but his reply was mild enough. "As you know, Tessa, *Empire* is on hiatus right now, so all the cast members are taking a break from filming. Jill was planning a trip to Alaska with some friends, and she seemed very excited about it last time we spoke."

The wry gleam of appreciation in Tessa's eyes acknowledged the skill with which Ben had avoided answering her real question, but she was a competent interviewer, and she quickly recovered her stride. "The rumor machine is grinding out word that *Empire* is going to finish the year with the cliff-hanger to end all cliff-hangers. We even heard that Harrison Brand might not survive into next season. Is there any truth to that rumor?"

Ben grinned. "Sounds to me as if my agent is working hard to get me a raise."

"So there's no truth to the recent reports that Harrison Brand dies in a parachute jump, attempting to rescue Sapphire and several other cast members from an Arab sheik's harem?"

"You know I can't give away any details of next season's story line, Tess. But I can tell you that I enjoy playing the part of Harrison Brand, and I don't think we've even begun to explore the full depth and range of his character. Speaking strictly personally, I'm hoping the writers and producers will allow his behavior to mature a little over the next few episodes."

"A tame Harrison Brand might not go over too well with *Empire*'s viewers."

"Harrison could never be tame." Ben's blue eyes twinkled. "But he's thirty-five years old and he's never been involved in a really serious relationship. I think it's time some woman introduced him to his fate, don't you? After all, *Empire* is the only one of the prime-time dramas that's never had a full-scale wedding written into its script."

Tessa was apparently well aware of the fact that she had just been thrown a major tidbit of information. "You're implying that Harrison Brand is going to be married next season. Is Sapphire the lucky woman who works the miracle of getting him to the altar?" she asked eagerly.

Ben smiled lazily. "Stay tuned," he said.

A frustrated but friendly sigh rippled through the listening crowd, and Laura realized that Ben had captured their attention with a completeness the vice president— or any other politican—might have envied. Tessa seemed to accept that she wasn't going to glean any further information about *Empire*'s story line, so she quickly changed the thrust of her questions.

"You're thirty-seven, Ben, a couple of years older than the character you play on television, and there've been some pretty wild incidents reported about your behavior in the past. You say it's time for Harrison Brand to mature, but what about you? Do you think you're finally mellowing out a little?"

"Could be. But my private life was never anywhere near as exciting as it sounded in the tabloids. I've often wished it was. On one occasion when we were on location, knee-deep in mud and mosquitoes, I remember reading that I'd been spotted swimming in a pool full of champagne, surrounded by bikini-clad starlets who were feeding me chocolate-covered strawberries. It sure sounded a great way to spend a hot afternoon."

"But it wasn't true?"

" 'Fraid not." He shrugged with almost comic regret, and even Tessa joined him in a rueful laugh.

"You've been a bachelor for several years now, Ben. Any chance that you might beat Harrison Brand to the altar?"

Ben gave another good-natured laugh. "That's an intriguing idea, and I'll certainly work on it. In theory, I've always thought marriage was a wonderful institution."

"But in practice?"

"In practice?" He paused for a moment, then shrugged, answering with unexpected seriousness. "In practice, I'm probably not an easy person to live with. I'd need a very strong and loving woman, with a high level of tolerance for my insecurities. Most actors have trouble identifying who they are when they're not playing a part, you know."

He glanced down at his watch, indifferent to the still-whirring camera. "You've had twelve minutes, Tess, two minutes more than we bargained for. I think I've earned free passage to your private dining room."

"I guess you have." Tessa gave a reluctant nod toward the technicians. "Okay, boys. Wind it up." She unpinned her mike and handed it to a waiting gofer. "Better move fast, Ben. Once the boys start taking down the barricades, we'll get trampled."

Ben turned around, gesturing to Laura and Christy to indicate they should follow, and all four of them walked quickly along the narrow pathway cleared by a couple of technicians.

Once they were safely inside the private dining room, Ben made the necessary introductions. "Tess, this is my daughter, Christy, and a friend of mine, Laura Forbes. This is Tessa Renier, Channel Eight's most talented reporter. We've known each other for nearly five years."

Christy shook hands, behaving very politely although she was obvioulsy simmering with repressed excitement. Laura shook hands, too, adding truthfully that she'd always admired Tessa's interviews on the nightly news.

The reporter's eyes narrowed thoughtfully. "Thanks. You must be from this area, if you watch our local news broadcasts. Have you and Ben known each other long?"

"Yes, I'm from Denver, but Ben and I only met—"

"Hey, Tess, give us all a break. The interview ended out there in the plaza." Ben dropped a casual arm around Laura's shoulders, creating a subtle aura of intimacy. She had the oddest feeling that he was creating the impression deliberately.

"We have to eat, Tessa," he explained. "Look at Christy! The poor kid's going to pass out in front of our eyes if she doesn't get some food soon."

"We climbed a mountain," Christy confided proudly. "Not quite to the top, but we got almost as far as the tree line. Would you like to have dinner with us, Tessa?"

The reporter glanced at her watch. "I'd love to, but I have to get those tapes back to Denver for editing. I'll send in a waitress for you on my way out. Watch the ten o'clock news tonight, Christy. You'll be able to see your dad *and* the vice president. That's quite a deal, huh?"

She turned to Laura, her expression still faintly speculative, though Ben had long since removed his arm. "Good-bye, Ms. Forbes. I'm only sorry we don't have more time to chat. Maybe we could have lunch some time?"

"Thank you, that would be very nice," Laura replied, feeling a certain wry amusement at the invitation. The reporter thought she scented a romance, and the more Laura protested that she and Ben were "only acquaintances," the more Tessa would suspect some secret relationship. Police work had shown Laura how easily false rumors could be started, but it was still somewhat unnerving to realize that she might find herself at the center of a juicy column in next week's supermarket tabloids. Oh, well, she thought. At least a report of her hot romance with Bennett Logan would make for a lighthearted moment in the dismal days ahead for her family.

Darkness fell long before they arrived back in Denver and the house was silent as they trooped into the kitchen from the garage. Laura was relieved to see no sign of Prudence Datscher. The immaculately groomed secretary always made her acutely aware of her own shortcomings, and at this precise moment she wasn't feeling in the mood to compare her unkempt appearance with Prudence's sleek perfection.

While Christy raided the refrigerator in search of an apple and a glass of milk, Laura slipped upstairs to the guest bedroom and took a quick shower, changing out of her grubby mountaineering outfit into a fresh pair of jeans and one of her favorite yellow cotton shirts.

As she hurried toward the bedroom door, she spied her cosmetic purse out of the corner of her eye. It looked very forlorn, sitting in the center of the huge dressing table, simply begging to be used.

She stopped in her tracks, hovering indecisively. Should she put on some makeup before she went downstairs? It was an uncharacteristic thought when she knew that in an hour's time—maybe less—she'd be coming upstairs to wash it all off again. She gave an impatient shrug. What had gotten into her? Why in the world would she consider putting on makeup at this hour of the night? She turned back toward the door.

But the dressing table and its fancy mirrors seemed to exert a compulsive fascination. Her mind carefully blank, Laura edged crabwise toward the corner of the room and sat down on the padded satin stool, staring into the lighted mirror. She scowled ferociously. No doubt about it, she looked every bit as boring as she'd expected. Healthy. There was simply no other word to describe her appearance.

She upended her cosmetic purse and examined the sparse contents, hovering in an odd state somewhere between tears and laughter. One pot of lip gloss, one mascara wand, one palette of eye shadow with a broken plastic lid, and a compact of powdered blush. Not exactly a stock of goodies calculated to turn a downy duckling into a sophisticated woman. Nevertheless, she smoothed tinted gloss onto her lips, brushed mauve eye shadow onto her eyelids, and darkened her lashes with mascara. The entire operation took about two minutes, which was twice as long as she usually spent in front of the mirror, even for special occasions.

Unfortunately, she decided, the extra minute was a wasted investment of her time, because she certainly didn't look twice as glamorous. She wrinkled her nose at her reflection, facing the truth. Even if she sucked in her cheeks and drooped her eyelashes seductively she was never going to bear any resemblance to elegant women like Prudence Datscher and Tessa Renier, much less to a steaming sexpot like Jill Cassell.

But my lashes are long—really long—and my mouth isn't so bad, she thought defiantly. She picked up her comb and ran it through her hair, grimacing as her curls bounced back into their usual soft brown mop. She pushed back the satin stool, astonished to find herself close to tears. What was the matter with her tonight? She thought she'd come to terms with her own asexual appearance years ago. Six years ago, to be precise, when her fiancé had walked out on her two days before their wedding.

She stuffed her makeup back into the purse and snapped off the lights around the mirror. You're dreaming dangerous dreams, she admonished herself. When the custody documents arrive from New York tomorrow, Bennett Logan will disappear from your life. You had a good time today . . . okay, so you had a terrific time . . . but if you don't want to get hurt, you'll remember this is simply a fun interlude. Don't ruin a pleasant set of memories by trying to turn these two days into something they're not.

Ben and Christy were waiting for her in the cathedral-ceilinged living room. He had changed into a dark blue track suit, and he, too, had obviously taken a shower because his thick blond hair was still damp in places. Laura felt her body's immediate response to his inherent sensuality, but she ruthlessly pushed the sensations away.

"Feeling sleepy?" she asked Christy.

"Mmm. Kind of. But I want to see the news. I've never seen myself on television before."

"Don't be disappointed if they didn't get you on camera," Ben said casually. "I think Tessa and I may have been standing at an angle that cut you out of range."

That had been a deliberate move on his part, Laura realized. She wondered if he'd ever received any actual kidnapping threats, since he really seemed more than usually uptight about keeping Christy out of the public eye.

"Would you like a glass of wine, Laura?" Ben gestured to a bottle of white Burgundy that sat in an ice bucket on the low table beside the sofa.

"Thank you." She accepted a glass and sat down on the sofa a safe distance from Ben.

"Have you ever been on television, Laura?" Christy asked.

"The back of my uniform a couple of times. Police officers and television news cameras often find themselves in the same place at the same time."

"What were you doing?" Christy asked with ghoulish interest. "Arresting a famous murderer?"

"No. I was helping ambulance crews pull drunken teenagers from wrecked cars. All police officers spend far too much time doing that."

"Oh." Christy pulled a face, her chastened expression turning to excitement as she watched the opening credits of the Channel 8 newscast. The presence of the vice president in Vail was the lead story, and she wriggled impatiently as the station's political commentator minutely analyzed the importance of his speech. Laura thought that if she'd been a few years younger, she'd have been wriggling, too.

Ben leaned back against the arm of the sofa and smothered a yawn. "I think I've finally wised up to the government's new foreign policy," he remarked during the station break. "They've given up trying to persuade us they're right, and now they're planning to bore us into agreement."

The advertisement for a local car dealership faded from the screen and was replaced by the Channel 8 anchorman. "The vice president wasn't Vail's only notable visitor this afternoon," he said, smiling toothily. "Bennett Logan, voted television's sexiest male star in this year's poll of viewers, was interviewed by our on-the-spot reporter, Tessa Renier. Over to you, Tessa."

Christy sat bolt upright on the edge of the sofa, her cheeks flushed bright red with the combination of excitement and mountain sun. "Looking good, Dad," she murmured tautly as Tessa's brief introduction faded into the actual tape of the interview.

"Thanks, honeybun." Ben sounded faintly amused

by his daughter's attempt at reassurance, and Laura could see the warmth of affection in his eyes as he turned to look at Christy.

The tape had been edited down to about four minutes, although the cuts were so cleverly made that most of Ben's answers remained intact. Tessa certainly knew her stuff, Laura acknowledged as the final few feet of tape played out and the camera began to pan the crowd.

Christy let out a little shriek of excitement. "There's me! There I am, Dad, right in front next to you! Can you see me?"

Ben swung his feet off the arm of the chair and stared intently at the screen. "Yes, I can see you." He drew in a deep breath, and to Laura it was obvious that he was forcing himself to remain calm. "With that purple hair it would be hard to miss you."

He picked up a remote-control device and pressed a few buttons. "I had the VCR running. Do you want to see yourself in instant replay?"

"Yes, please," Christy responded at once, too young for any display of false modesty. "It's fun seeing yourself on television, isn't it, Laura?"

Ben looked as if he thought the experience was anything but fun. He really is overreacting, Laura thought. After all, a brief glimpse of Christy on-screen surely wasn't going to have kidnappers and extortionists descending in droves on the Logan residence. Relatively speaking, Denver wasn't much of a center for organized crime and the tape wasn't likely to get any airplay outside of Colorado. She looked closely at the videotaped images. In fact, although the camera had honed in on Christy for a closeup, there was no way an outsider could tell that she had any special connection to Ben. She was about to make some comment to this effect when Christy spoke again.

"I can see you, too, Laura. Look, there's a really

good shot of you. Do you realize you're only a few inches taller than me?"

Ben obligingly froze the frame on the screen, and Laura studied herself with a heady mixture of fascination and embarrassment. The television lens had captured a different image from the one she was familiar with, and she hardly recognized the slender, dark-eyed vibrant woman on the screen.

"You look nice," Christy said. "But you're even prettier in real life."

The compliment was all the more compelling for being handed out so casually. Christy seemed to consider her words so self-evidently true that she didn't even wait for Laura's response. "Dad, could you reverse the tape so we can see it again?"

He pressed the button for rewind. "You just want to admire your purple hair," he teased.

"No," she replied seriously. "I like watching you as well as me. When Mom wouldn't let me come to visit you, I used to watch *Empire* every week. But on the show you were always pretending to be somebody else, not my father, and it was sort of strange. When you talked to that reporter, you seemed kind of halfway between my father and the person I've been watching on TV. It sort of helps me to join the two pieces of you up together again, if you know what I mean."

Christy was an exceptionally perceptive child, Laura thought, turning away as Ben got up from his chair and gathered his daughter into a tight, emotion-packed hug.

"Dad, promise you won't let her take me away again?" Christy's face was buried tight in her father's shoulder and her plea was barely audible.

His face was somber as he repeated the promise he'd made the night before. "Trust me, honey. Nobody's going to take you away from me ever again."

Neither of them looked up as Laura quietly eased herself off the sofa and left the room.

Chapter Five

THE EXPRESS PACKAGE arrived from New York at nine-thirty the next morning. Ben strode into the living room, slitting open the envelope as he came.

"Here," he said briskly, pulling out a bundle of documents and handing them to Laura without even bothering to glance down. He skimmed his lawyer's accompanying letter, then handed her that, too. "Aaron is usually very efficient. I hope he's sent everything you need."

He sounded cool, crisp, studiously polite—and obviously burning with impatience for her to be gone. She couldn't blame him, of course. From his point of view she'd been hanging around, intruding on his reunion with Christy, and all for the sake of a legal formality he no doubt considered utterly trivial. Looked at from his perspective, he had been remarkably kind. His manner had always been scrupulously polite and sometimes downright friendly. He'd even thrown in a couple of Hollywood-style kisses just so she would have some-

thing exciting to reminisce about when she talked over
the incident with her envious colleagues. Laura felt her
cheeks grow hot as she remembered her passionate response to Ben's casual embrace, and she bent her head
quickly to scan the crucial documents.

The lawyer's covering letter, typed on heavyweight
cream paper, was only three sentences long:

> *Dear Ben: Here are the documents you re-
> quested. Hope you're having a good time out
> there in the boonies, although I can't understand
> why you want to surround yourself with all that
> gruesome untamed nature. When are you coming
> back to civilization? Regards, Aaron P. Schrenk.*

"Don't be offended by his opinion of Colorado," Ben
said as she set the letter down on the escritoire.
"Aaron's convinced the Wild West starts in the middle
of the Hudson River and stretches clear over to San
Francisco. He probably thinks hardware stores in
Denver do a brisk trade in arrows and tomahawks."

She smiled. "I know how he feels. My brothers believe real, honest-to-God America vanishes at the Iowa
state line." Laura unfolded the sheaf of papers that accompanied the lawyer's letter. On top of the pile was a
notarized copy of Ben's four-and-a-half-year-old divorce decree. Just as he had claimed, custody of Christy
Annabell Logan had been jointly awarded to both parents. No specific schedule of visits had been set up, but
the court admonished the divorcing couple to set aside
their differences and work out a living arrangement that
would prove of maximum benefit to their child.

Another document clipped into the file proved
slightly more surprising. It showed that Ben was not
obligated to pay his ex-wife any alimony. He was, however, required to make extremely generous child-support

payments during the time that Christy lived with her mother.

Judges and lawyers were not always as wise as they might be, Laura reflected. Any police officer or social worker would have realized immediately that a huge financial settlement tied to a vague custody arrangement was guaranteed to cause strife. In effect, the judge's decision meant that Renee's income ballooned whenever Christy was living with her, and disappeared if Christy lived with her father. The mystery of why Renee insisted on keeping her daughter was now solved. Having a rebellious teenager around the house probably seemed a small price to pay in exchange for thousands of dollars in monthly child-support income.

However, Ben and Renee's financial hassles were none of Laura's business, and since Ben had provided proof of his unrestricted right to custody, there was no reason why she shouldn't leave Christy in his care. All in all, the outcome was better than she could have dreamed when she first stopped outside the Galaxy Video Arcade and took an exhausted, purple-haired runaway into her charge.

She was feeling terrific about everything, Laura assured herself. Absolutely terrific. Except that she got this uncomfortable niggle in the pit of her stomach every time she looked at the documents. The prickly sort of niggle that police officers learned to ignore at their peril.

She ran her finger over the embossed notary's seal and scrutinized the divorce decree one final time. There seemed no doubt at all that the documents were genuine. The humiliating thought occurred to her that she was subconsciously searching for excuses to spend more time in Ben's company. As soon as that thought crystallized in her mind, she gathered up the sheaf of papers with exaggerated briskness and closed the folder with a definite snap.

She handed the whole package back to Ben, smiling with cool, professional courtesy. "Everything seems in perfect order. I'm sorry I couldn't take your word for things, but you'll understand that in police business, we have to go by the letter of the law."

"Of course I understand." His answering smile was warm, charming—and something else she couldn't quite identify. He tossed the papers onto the escritoire and took her hand in a friendly shake. His expression became faintly teasing, and totally irresistible. "You've taught me to be a reformed citizen, Laura. In future, I promise to keep copies of my important personal records in my home as well as in my lawyer's office."

"That's always a good idea. You never know when somebody might need to refer to them." She turned away, knowing how prim she sounded but helpless to change it. She'd never been any good at witty, meaning-less repartee.

"Well, I know Prudence has a long list of chores waiting for me, so if you'll excuse me, Laura, I'll go and report for duty. I already asked Juan to bring the Mercedes around to the front driveway. I'm sure you must be anxious to get home."

It was a little more subtle than kicking her out of the door, Laura thought wryly, but not much. "My bags are in the hall," she said. "If Juan's ready right now, I'd appreciate a ride home."

"Of course, he'll be happy to take you. After the L.A. freeways, he considers driving in Denver the next best thing to a vacation."

They both started toward the doorway at the same time and for a moment they were no more than inches apart. Ben stared down at her, his blue eyes gleaming with something close to regret.

"Christy and I both had a great time yesterday," he said after a tiny pause. "You're an outstanding person to climb a mountain with."

"Thanks." She cleared her throat in an attempt to cover her sudden breathlessness. "You're not such a slouch yourself."

He tipped his hand to his forehead in mock salute. "Thanks for everything, Laura. Take care when you're out there keeping the streets safe for honest citizens." Without a backward glance he strode down the hallway in the direction of his secretary's office.

"Hey, wait a minute, Dad, don't go! What's happening?" Christy tumbled out of the den, where she had been holed up since breakfast exploring the wonders of her father's record collection.

"Laura's getting ready to leave."

"To leave?"

"Duty calls," Laura said lightly. "I report back to work tomorrow morning and I have a dozen chores I need to get done this afternoon." She gave Christy a quick hug, feeling the tension in the girl's too-thin shoulders and sensing that tears were not far away. She drew back in exaggerated astonishment. "Ouch! Your bones just dug into me! I don't know where you put all that food you eat, kiddo. You must have a pair of hollow legs."

Christy managed a pale smile. "Nope. Dad says I take after him. I use up a lot of nervous energy."

Laura's gaze softened. "Maybe you'll relax a little more, now that you're here in Denver with your father. Have a good summer, Christy. I'm glad things worked out so well for you."

"But why do you have to leave right now? You're not working until tomorrow, so couldn't you stay for lunch at least?"

Of course she could, if she really wanted to. If Ben wanted her to. Laura sneaked a look at Ben, who appeared to be lost in contemplation of the skylight. His pointed indifference stiffened her resolve. "Sorry, kiddo, but I have a couple of pressing errands to run this afternoon. I'm sure you and your dad will be able to figure out something exciting to do after he's finished work." She bent down and picked up her two small backpacks. "Have fun in summer school, Christy. Don't worry, you'll soon make a whole bunch of interesting new friends."

Christy's mouth tightened into a stubborn line. "If you can't stay for lunch today, why don't you come back for dinner tomorrow night?"

"I'm working a shift and a half tomorrow," Laura said gently. Seeing Christy's crestfallen expression, she attempted a feeble joke. "Somebody has to watch out for the runaways on Colfax Avenue, you know."

Christy didn't even smile. "Then come back over the weekend," she said. "Please, Laura, I really want to see you again. Wouldn't you like to share a pizza with my dad and me? I thought you liked us."

"I do like you, of course I do." Laura sighed inwardly. She had worked with enough teenagers to realize why Christy was being so persistent. Laura represented the only link between her old life and the new one she had run away to find. More uncertain than she dared to admit, Christy was clinging to that link with a tenacity that was out of proportion to the importance Laura really held in her life.

In other circumstances Laura wouldn't have hesitated to accept Christy's repeated invitations, knowing that the girl would forget all about her as soon as she enrolled in school and met other teenagers. Unfortunately, Ben's manner made it all too obvious that he didn't want Laura to return to his house. Which meant that she faced a difficult choice—she could annoy Ben or disappoint Christy.

Out of the corner of her eye she saw that Ben had stopped staring at the skylight. He walked down the hallway toward them both and she looked at him questioningly, conveying the silent message that she wasn't going to accept Christy's invitation without his explicit consent.

He stopped when he was still a couple of feet away from them, shoving his hands into the pockets of his slacks. He spoke abruptly, his words clipped. "Please do join us for a pizza on Sunday evening, Laura. You may as well make life easier for all of us and say yes right away. Once my daughter gets an idea into her head, she sticks to it like a limpet."

He couldn't have sounded less enthusiastic without being openly rude, and if she had even a grain of common sense, she would say no. Laura looked from Ben's unsmiling profile to Christy's pleading, heart-shaped face and felt her good resolutions crumble. Christy was just a child, a scared child who was feeling extremely insecure. She, on the other hand, was supposed to be a mature adult who surely ought to be able to handle a little coolness from her TV heartthrob for the length of time it took to consume a couple of slices of pizza. What was Ben so uptight about, after all? Did he expect her to fall on him and demand an instant replay of the kiss by the waterfall? If so, she would soon set his mind at rest. She was probably as anxious as he was to keep their relationship on an impersonal basis. After all, she was the one who would end up hurt if she ever allowed her deeper feelings to be touched.

"Well, all right, Christy," she said finally. "If you really want me to come and if *you* don't mind, Ben . . ."

"Why should I mind?" He gave an odd little laugh. "Pizza has always been one of my favorite foods, ever since I worked my way through college sprinkling mozzarella and mushrooms onto Gino's Famous Pizzas."

She hadn't been asking whether or not he liked pizza and they both knew it, but Laura decided not to comment on his answer.

"I'm working a split shift, but I could be here by eight, if that's convenient for you both."

Christy was delighted. "Any time's convenient, isn't it, Dad? Are you sure you can't make it any earlier?" She didn't wait for an answer, hopping with enthusiasm as she accompanied Laura to the front door. "We'll order an extra-large pizza with a thick crust and every-thing on it, except maybe anchovies and olives. How about double cheese? Would you like to have double cheese?"

"Sounds irresistible. I'm hungry already."

"Great! Then we'll see you on Sunday. It'll be fun, you'll see." Christy swung open the front door. As re-luctant as most teenagers to demonstrate affection, she gave Laura's hand a furtive, embarrassed squeeze. "Thanks for everything," she whispered. "I'm really grateful for all you did."

By exercising superhuman self-discipline, Laura managed to avoid asking Juan a single question about his employer during the entire ride home. Instead, they discussed the tribulations of the Denver Zephyrs and the iniquities of the baseball commissioner, who had once again refused to authorize a major league baseball team for the Mile High City.

She soon began to regret her choice of conversation, since Juan found the subject of baseball so enthralling that he did most of his driving with no hands on the steering wheel. Closing her eyes so she wouldn't have to see what was flashing past the car window, she pointed out to him that, although Denver highways might seem tame in comparison to Los Angeles free-ways, they still carried enough traffic to kill a person very dead.

Juan shrugged indifferently, assuring her that he had never been involved in even the least significant of acci-dents. "All my passengers arrive home very safe," he said, beaming into the rearview mirror and immediately

renewing his slanderous attack on the morals and man-
hood of the baseball commissioner.

He parted from Laura with many compliments, going
so far as to say what a pleasure it was to chauffeur a
woman who was smart enough to be more interested in
baseball than in the love life of his employer.

If only he knew, Laura thought wryly, letting herself
into her apartment. She dumped her backpacks on the
living room sofa and disciplined her mind to shut out all
thought of Bennett Logan. The past two days had been a
pleasant interlude, but now it was time to return to the
real world. She decided that if she concentrated on
thinking sensible thoughts for the next seventy years or
so, she would probably forget all about Ben in good
time to celebrate her hundredth birthday.

The letter from her brother, David, was still sitting
on the bed where she had thrown it. She picked it up,
her stomach churning with a helpless mixture of love
and guilt as she read it over once again. It was bad
enough to live with the knowledge that her family was
about to go under. It was even worse that she should be
here in Denver, so comfortable and so separate from
their undeserved failure.

There was no longer any point in practicing petty
economies in her budget, so she picked up the phone
and dialed home. Everybody was there, and everybody
wanted to speak to her. Everybody was also determined
to pretend that nothing was wrong, until Laura could
stand the kind, well-meant lies no longer.

"What's going to happen, Jim?" she asked bluntly.
"Is the bank still going to foreclose at the end of the
month?"

Silence descended, and she felt the despair reaching
out over six hundred miles of telephone wire. "The
bank's calling the loan at the end of the month," her
brother admitted finally. "Dave and I spoke to the manager and asked him to hold off until we'd finished the

summer harvest, but he says his hands are tied. The directors insist the bank's debts are too high and they're calling in every loan over thirty thousand."

"You know I have that thousand dollars I was saving—"

"Don't even mention it," Jim cut in. "You've already sent us far more than we want to take from you. Don't worry, Laurie-love, things'll work out."

Her breath caught harshly in her throat. "Oh, Jim, I don't see how! At least let me send you something to help out with the move and everything."

She could sense the effort with which he lightened his tone of voice. "We're not penniless, Laurie, only bankrupt! The bank manager tells me that's not quite the same thing."

"But I don't need the money right now—"

"You listen to me, girl. You save that money for your hope chest, and when you marry some fancy Denver dude, we'll all come and dance at your wedding."

Her face was stiff with the effort of holding back her tears. "Right, we'll plan on it, Jim. Before the summer's over for sure."

"Does that mean you have somebody lined up already? Hey, did you hear that, Mom? Laurie's found herself a new beau and she's planning on marrying this one!"

Laura swallowed hard, drawing on reserves of fortitude she hadn't known she possessed. If Jim could be cheerful, so could she, even if the effort damn near killed her. "You don't know the half of it. Tell Mom I'm flying in high circles these days. You'll never guess where I spent my day off this week."

"Where?"

"Climbing a mountain with Mr. Bennett Logan. *The* Bennett Logan, in fact."

As she had intended, her statement provoked a storm of excited questions, and she launched into a deliberately humorous version of her encounter with Ben, squeezing every possible ounce of glamor from the brief time they had spent together. Her family laughed a lot, although the laughter sometimes sounded perilously strained, and her mother came onto the line to say that she still had a hat left over from Jim's wedding fifteen years earlier, so she was all prepared if Laurie wanted to set an early date for her marriage to Bennett Logan.

When Laura finally hung up the phone, she was so proud of her family, and so sorry for them, that she didn't know whether she wanted to laugh, or to cry, or to storm around the apartment smashing things. In the end, being a sensible, self-controlled woman, she did none of those things. Instead, she watered her plants and applied herself diligently to the mundane tasks of sorting her laundry, going grocery shopping, and polishing her furniture.

In view of her exemplary self-discipline, she considered it a lowdown trick of fate when she curled up on the sofa to watch an hour of television and realized that it was Thursday night—and the season finale of *Empire*.

With a sigh of guilty pleasure, Laura leaned back against the cushions and watched Harrison Brand swing into heart-stopping, pulse-quickening action. Last week his mistress, the beautiful Sapphire Steddon, had disappeared into the harem of the evil, warmongering Sheik of Drabu'an. In this week's episode, government officials in Washington were holding hurried conferences and concocting desperate rescue plans to get Sapphire back. For Sapphire, the scriptwriters revealed with a flourish, was not only the possessor of the most sensuous body outside the pages of *Playboy* magazine, she was also the possessor of the most brilliant mind since Albert Einstein. Her disappearance threatened to set back America's laser research by at least a decade, and the Pentagon was holding Harrison Brand personally responsible for her kidnapping.

"Sapphire would never have been captured if that damned sex maniac hadn't addled her wits," a four-star general complained. "What the hell has he done to her?"

"Taken her to bed and spent the whole night making love?" a female agent suggested helpfully.

The general's mustache bristled with outrage. "What's that got to do with anything? Sapphire's supposed to be a trained scientist, but ever since she met Harrison Brand she's behaved just like any other woman. I swear she's bewitched."

I can relate to that, Laura thought wryly as the scene switched to Cairo, where Harrison Brand had flown on the first stage of his personal rescue mission. She watched, half laughing, half caught up in the absurd story, as two Pentagon officials forced their way into his hotel bedroom, intent on arresting him.

The producers of the show took full advantage of their photo opportunity and ordered up several lingering shots of an adorably rumpled—and obviously nude—Harrison Brand. The agents marched across the room as Harrison rose slowly from his bed, the camera angles giving fifty million female viewers a wonderful view of his gleaming pectorals and flat stomach muscles while still keeping him just on the right side of television decency codes.

Harrison, looking relaxed and confident, smiled with mocking courtesy as he greeted the agents. The agents, looking uncomfortably overdressed in their gray pinstripes, announced that he was under arrest. Harrison showed no sign of dismay, although his smile became a shade more mocking. The veteran of a dozen hair-raising bedroom escapes, his casual manner suggested that he was unlikely to be trapped by a couple of bureaucrats freshly unwound from the red tape of the Pentagon hierarchy.

Laura stared at Harrison as he negligently gathered up a sheet and twisted it around his waist. For an instant her heart seemed to stop beating. Then it rushed forward again at twice its normal speed. The ridiculous story line suddenly seemed less than amusing. A sharp, bittersweet memory of Ben's kiss superimposed itself over the unrealistic television images and she felt a wave of desire so intense that her fists clenched involuntarily among the sofa cushions.

As soon as she was aware of what she was doing, she uncurled her fingers and turned away from the screen to plump up the pillows. She padded into the kitchen and checked her coffee supply for the morning, then drank a glass of water she didn't really want. When she returned to the living room, she had lost track of what was happening on screen, but she watched in reluctant fascination as Harrison, now dressed in jeans and an unbuttoned shirt, made good his escape. He jumped over a strategically placed armchair, flashed a final impudent grin toward the bumbling agents, and hightailed it out of the bedroom window.

The show's final shot showed him parachuting into the harem compound of the Sheik of Drabu'an — as a platoon of black-robed guards moved in silently for the kill.

"Crazy, ridiculous episode," Laura muttered as she flicked off the switch on the TV. "I'm not even going to watch this show next season, it's too silly." She marched into her bedroom and set her alarm for five o'clock, then climbed into bed and rolled over onto her stomach, composing herself for sleep.

An hour had gone by before she realized why sleep was proving so elusive. Harrison Brand's smile! She sat bolt upright in bed, staring into the darkness, all trace of sleepiness vanished. The triumphant smile he had flashed in the direction of the outwitted Pentagon agents was identical to the smile Bennett Logan had shot at Laura when she accepted the validity of his custody documents.

She hoped very much that the similarity was purely coincidental. Police instinct warned her that it wasn't.

Chapter Six

THE NEXT THREE days made Laura wonder why she had ever decided to become a law enforcement officer. On Friday she supervised the aftermath of two traffic accidents, then rounded off her shift by answering a call from an elderly man who had lost his life savings in a burglary. Saturday was even worse, with the entire miserable day punctuated by the arrest of drunks, small-time crooks, and street-corner drug pushers.

By the middle of her shift on Sunday she was emotionally exhausted. Early that morning she had picked up another runaway on Colfax Avenue. Young Derek was caught stealing cigarettes, and he hadn't been home in two weeks. Laura escorted him back to his parents' apartment, but his father and stepmother refused point blank to allow him through the door.

"He stole money from my purse," his stepmother said, not bothering to take her cigarette from her mouth while she spoke. "He's trouble. By all accounts he's bin nothin' but trouble from the day he was born."

His father concurred. "You keep him at the police station and see's if you can knock some sense into him. I ain't had no luck and God knows I tried. There ain't nobody as can say 1 ain't done my share in raisin' him." He shut the door and slammed home the bolt.

Laura silently indicated that Derek should return to the squad car. She had no doubt that his mother was telling the truth about the stolen money, but her heart ached for the bitter hurt she could see reflected in the boy's eyes. She bought him a hamburger and a soda as they rode back to the police station, forcing herself to ignore the running stream of verbal abuse he kept up as she contacted the juvenile welfare department. When a social worker came to take him into custody, she handed Derek a slip of paper with her phone number written on it.

"Give me a call if you think I can help," she said quietly.

"Yeah, sure thing, police lady." Derek hooked his thumbs into his belt and smirked sarcastically, adding a string of obscene suggestions to round out his reply. He stopped abruptly. "You won't be there," he said. "If I called, you wouldn't be there."

"Maybe not," she said gently. "I have to work most days. But if I'm not home, leave a message on my answering machine. I always reply to my phone calls, Derek, and that's a promise."

He looked at her in silence for a long time, then turned and jerked his head insolently at the social worker. "Let's go, big guy. Watcha standing around for, anyways? You got the hots for Ms. Police Lady here, or somethin'?"

Laura watched Derek leave, her mouth dry with the awareness of failure. She hoped against hope that a foster home would eventually be found for him, but she wasn't optimistic. She knew as well as every other police officer that sixteen-year-old boys with lousy school records and rebellious attitudes usually graduated straight from juvenile group homes into adult prisons. The waste of it all tore at her gut.

She had five minutes before her shift ended so she scrawled herself a few notes about Derek's case, then reached into her overflowing desk drawer and pulled out Christy's file. She dialed Renee Logan's number in California, letting the phone ring a dozen times before she gave up and replaced the receiver. The file would just have to remain on the active list for another couple of days until she managed to notify the former Mrs. Logan that Christy had been returned to her father's care.

Laura slipped Christy's folder into her desk and headed for the parking lot. Tonight she would be seeing Ben again, and her heart gave a ridiculous little lurch of excitement. For at least the tenth time, she reminded herself that the dinner invitation came from Christy, not from Ben, so there was no valid reason for the bubbling sense of anticipation fizzing inside her.

In any case, she mocked herself, what was she hoping would happen tonight? Were her fantasies so out of control that she expected Ben to stage a grand seduction scene and whiz her into his bed for a night of wild, uninhibited sex? The thought was absurd enough to make her smile. On a sensuality scale of one to ten, her rating couldn't possibly be more than a minus three. Even dear old Russ, her fiancé, had complained that making love to her was about as exciting as going to bed with a pair of fluffy slippers. Despite those two kisses Ben had exchanged with her, Laura doubted if he altogether realized she was a functioning female. Why should he? No other man did, although they frequently told her what a wonderful friend she was, and what a good sport, and how much they wished their wives and/or girl friends were as understanding as she.

Laura slammed the door of her car and edged out into the stream of Sunday evening traffic. Of course she knew that a one-night stand with Bennett Logan was likely to cause her nothing but heartache. Of course she was far too sensible and mature to want to indulge in casual sex. But just for once, she thought wistfully, it would be wonderful to know that a man like Ben found her desirable.

Laura glanced ruefully into the rearview mirror, then switched lanes. Perhaps it was just as well that the chances of her being invited into Ben's bed were close to zero. With the strange mood she found herself in these days, she was crazy enough to accept, and she would undoubtedly live to regret such impetuosity. If she wanted to avoid getting hurt, she knew how she had to behave tonight. She would be friendly to Christy, appreciative of the pizza, and politely aloof from the dazzling effects of Bennett Logan's smile.

The advice was first-rate, but Laura soon discovered she was in no mood to heed her own warnings. She came out of the shower and defiantly rubbed the steam away from the bathroom mirror. Remaining politely aloof, she decided, didn't mean that she had to turn up tonight looking like a dowd. Just because she wasn't a hot candidate for a frolic in Ben's bed didn't mean that she had to go around looking like a reject from the Miss Iowa Cornhusking Pageant. Her body might not be tall and sleek, but she had a decent figure—long legs, slim waist, curvaceous breasts—and it was about time she started flaunting some of her attributes. After all, even the luscious Sapphire would never have captured anybody's attention if she'd stayed hidden behind her lab coats, devoting all her energy to the study of laser beams.

Laura spent twenty minutes experimenting with her hair dryer and discovered that, with concentration, it was possible to style her tangle of curls into a gleaming cap of golden brown hair. Encouraged by her unexpected success with the dryer, she applied her makeup more boldly than usual, brushing on lipstick, blush, and eyeshadow, then thickening her long lashes with two coats of mascara. When she was through, she was secretly pleased by the overall effect, although she was relieved none of her colleagues from vice were around to pass any ribald comments.

She zipped up her jeans and reached for a clean cotton T-shirt, but somehow her hand landed on an aquamarine blouse that was tucked away at the back of the closet. She slipped it on, tying the sash at the waist, relishing the cold, slithery feel of the satin against her skin. Her breath caught tight in her throat when she glimpsed herself in the mirror. Not bad, kid, she told her reflection. In this blouse you might even *win* the Miss Iowa Cornhusking Pageant.

The night air still carried a hint of afternoon warmth when she rang the doorbell at Ben's house. The last chime had scarcely died away when Christy pulled open the front door.

"Laura—at last! We've been expecting you for *ages*. We called for the pizza already and it'll be here in ten minutes. I hope you're hungry, because we ordered the super giant size."

Her enthusiasm was contagious and, for the first time, Laura felt unreservedly glad she'd come. It was crazy to deprive herself of the pleasure of Christy's company just because she was afraid of her infatuation with Christy's father. She gave the teenager a tiny hug and a big smile.

"Ten whole minutes before we get to eat, huh? Let's hope I survive that long. Lunch didn't make it onto my schedule today and I'm starving."

"I am, too, but I'm always starving. Come on in. Hey, that shirt's a great color! Oh, here's my dad. Don't you like Laura's shirt, Dad? She looks terrific, doesn't she?"

"Just terrific," Ben said smoothly. "Nice to see you again, Laura. How are you doing?"

"Fine, thanks. Looking forward to our pizza since I missed lunch."

His mouth quirked up in the grin that always turned her weak at the knees. "Have the bad guys been keeping you too busy to eat?"

"The bad guys and the lunatics who insist on drinking before they get behind the wheels of their cars. I'm getting tired of holding IVs while the paramedics try to pry mangled bodies out of wrecked vehicles."

His eyes darkened with immediate sympathy. "I'm sorry. It sounds like you've had a rough three days. Come and sit down, you need to unwind." He took her hand, holding it casually as he led her into the living room.

"Like a beer?" he asked as she settled herself on the sofa.

"Thanks, that sounds good."

He walked over to a corner bar and popped open the top on a can of light ale. "Need a glass?"

She shook her head and he opened another can, carrying them both across to where she and Christy were seated. He handed her one of the beers, then sat down in a nearby armchair, stretching his legs out in front of him.

Christy prodded him affectionately. "Don't get too comfortable, Dad, or you'll fall asleep."

He yawned. "Too true. I've just spent three days discovering how exhausting it is to be the father of a teenager."

"What have you done to wear your father out?" Laura asked, laughing. "Something fun, I'll bet. You have a brand-new suntan, Christy, and it suits you."

"We went to Estes Park on Friday and yesterday we went water-skiing at Chatfield Reservoir." She giggled. "Dad wore sunglasses and an orange wig so nobody would recognize him. Can you imagine what we looked like skiing together?"

Ben grinned lazily. "Two Bozo the Clowns in swimsuits, according to my secretary. She definitely didn't approve. But the really amazing thing is that I skied for three hours and didn't lose my wig in the water. Nobody seems suitably impressed by my great achievement."

"I'm impressed," Laura said. "Wasn't the water horribly cold?"

"Freezing," Ben replied affably. "I'm probably suffering from the early stages of pneumonia as well as the final stages of terminal exhaustion."

Laura watched as father and daughter exchanged intimate, comfortable smiles. No wonder Christy had been so anxious to get back to Denver, she thought. She and her father had an exceptionally warm and relaxed relationship for two people who had been separated for almost four years.

The doorbell rang. "I'll get it," Christy said. "If you go, Dad, they'll expect you to stand there for hours signing autographs. All I'll have to do is pay."

"Don't forget the tip," Ben called after her. He got up from his chair to open another beer. "Want another?" he asked Laura.

She shook her head and he walked over to a nearby window, drawing back the drapes so that he could sit on the cushioned window ledge. "I half expected to get a phone call from you," he said after a little pause.

"A phone call?"

"About Christy. To let me know that the paperwork was in order and the case was closed. That sort of thing."

"Unfortunately, the paperwork isn't finished yet."

"The bad guys keeping you permanently away from your desk as well as from lunch?"

"Yes, but that's not the reason the file's still open. Christy left California without permission from her legal guardian, which means I have to make contact with your former wife to tell her where Christy ended up. So far, I've had no luck in reaching her, either at her hotel in New York or at her home number in California."

"According to Christy, it'll be at least another week before Renee leaves New York." Ben took a long swallow from his can of beer. "I could have my lawyers contact Renee on your behalf, if you like. I have several things to discuss with her anyway, and it would save you the trouble of constantly calling long distance."

His offer was so carefully casual that every niggle of doubt Laura had ever felt came rushing back in a single swoop of suspicion. "Calling Christy's mother is no trouble," she said, getting up and walking over to the window. "What is it, Ben? What are you afraid I'll find out when I get in touch with your ex-wife?"

"Why, nothing at all, Laura. What could there possibly be to find out?" His blue eyes gazed deep into hers, brilliant in their sincerity. He allowed the drape to fall back into place and touched her lightly on the end of her nose. "Your police person instincts are getting the better of your common sense, Sergeant Forbes."

She moved away from the temptation of his touch. "No," she replied quietly. "My police person instincts are finally responding the way they should have five days ago."

"Laura, think about what you're saying. If I had anything to hide, why would I hang around in Denver? Christy and I could have been out of here half an hour after you left the house."

"That's true," she said, forcing herself not to respond to the husky appeal in his voice. "But I've been a cop for five years and I know when people are lying to me. You're nervous as hell about something, Ben, and I'd like to know what it is."

He studied her intently for several seconds, his expression revealing absolutely nothing. "Laura," he said finally, "after four years of trailing around with her mother, Christy needs stability in her life. Would you hel—"

"Here it is!" Christy returned to the room carrying a huge cardboard container. "Sorry to have been so long. The delivery man had the orders all mixed up, but we straightened it out and I tipped him two dollars like you said, Dad."

She set the carton in the center of the coffee table and flung open the lid. Oregano-scented steam rose in enticing waves from the mounds of tomato sauce and mozzarella cheese. "Mmm, the world's best smell," she said, upending a paper bag next to the box of pizza. "Here's napkins, plates, and plastic forks if you want them. Go ahead, Laura, choose the first piece, since you're the guest and you didn't get to eat lunch."

Laura took a well-smothered slice and maneuvered it onto a paper plate without losing any of the topping and without getting any sauce on her fingers.

"A certified pizza expert," Ben murmured.

"I have years of practice. Eating take-out food with one hand is a required course for all rookies and if you want to make detective, you have to be able to answer the phone, write out a report, and eat pizza all at the same time. I'm getting so good, I'm just about ready to demand a promotion."

Ben laughed. "Sounds as if police work is like the acting profession. What you really need to become a star isn't so much talent as a cast-iron digestive system."

Christy finished her first slice of pizza and reached for a second. "You may have a cast-iron stomach, Dad, but I think you're a terrific actor, too. Did you watch *Empire* the other night, Laura? Wasn't it exciting?"

"Very exciting, and I read the next day that it swept the ratings."

"I liked it when Harrison escaped from the Pentagon

agents by jumping out the window. Which part did you like best?"

"I guess I liked the bit where all those pistol-toting, saber-swishing guards were closing in ready to kill your father."

Ben feigned exaggerated dismay. "Please, Sergeant Forbes, watch what you're saying! I detect some distinctly Freudian undertones in that reply. You might at least remember to say you liked the bit where the guards were moving in to kill *Harrison Brand*." He leaned back against the cushions, his expression suddenly serious. "We're not the same person, you know, and I wish more people would remember that."

"Oh, Dad! Of course Laura knows you're only acting a part on TV, just like she knows the guards aren't really going to kill you." Christy leaned forward confidingly. "Next season Dad's going to rescue Sapphire from the sheik's harem, but he isn't going to marry her. He's going to fall in love with this doctor in the hospital where he goes to recuperate from his saber wounds. Dad showed me a photo of the woman who's going to play the doctor, and she's kind of geeky-looking, not a bit like Sapphire. But Dad says it's going to be a very touching love story."

"Well, bang goes the secret of the entire plot line for next season," Ben said wryly. "Do you happen to remember, honeybun, that I told you all that information was strictly confidential?"

"But I only told Laura." Christy stopped eating pizza just long enough to look hurt. "She doesn't count as a regular person, does she? I wouldn't have told anybody who mattered, like a reporter or anything."

Ben winced. "Before you get up and leave, Laura, I think my daughter was intending to pay you a compliment."

"It sure sounded like one to me," Laura replied,

smiling. "So what else did you do this weekend, Christy?"

There was a pause while she wiped each of her fingers on a napkin. "Dad made me register for school," she said at last. "We went together on Friday morning, and I guess it didn't look like too bad a place. For a school."

"Well, that's really good news. Congratulations, Christy. When do you start?"

"Tomorrow," she replied gloomily. "The counselor thought I might as well finish up the year even though there are only a few weeks left to go. This way, I'll have a better idea what courses I need to take in summer school." She fiddled nervously with one of the plastic forks. "I hope the other kids aren't too mean. The ones I saw all looked kind of stuck-up."

"Keep a low profile and concentrate on getting to know one or two people really well," Ben advised. "There are bound to be a few kids in your classes who are willing to make friends."

"I guess so." Christy stacked used paper plates and plastic forks into the empty pizza carton, her mind clearly not on her task. "I wish my hair was just a regular color," she burst out finally. "Nobody in Denver has purple hair. The kids at school will think I'm a freak."

"Tell them what you told us," Laura suggested. "Explain that you lived in England for a while, and that's where you learned to dye your hair. The other students will probably be quite impressed."

"They're more likely to think I'm a geek."

"Not once they see how well you can play tennis," Ben said reassuringly. "When you've helped the tennis team win a few tournaments, you'll find nobody pays any attention to the color of your hair."

Christy looked less than convinced. "It's almost the end of the season. They probably won't even let me try out for the team." She fiddled with a discarded crust of

pizza. "I'm getting butterflies in my stomach just thinking about tomorrow. I wish it was morning already so
that I could get it over and done with."

"Maybe you'd better have an early night in bed,"
Ben suggested. "Remember you have to catch the
school bus at seven-thirty."

Laura expected a storm of protest, but to her surprise, Christy got meekly to her feet and yawned
widely. "Sounds like a great idea, Dad. I think I might
go up to my room right now. I'm kind of tired and I
have to decide which of my new outfits I'm going to
wear tomorrow. I'm sorry to run out on you so soon,
Laura, but would you mind if I left you and my dad to
keep each other company? I'm sure the two of you can
find lots to talk about."

Laura glanced up at Christy's all-too-transparent face
and felt her heart plummet. Having dealt with so many
teenagers, she knew exactly what the poor girl was trying to do. Having decided that Laura was an okay sort
of person, Christy was now attempting a little match-
making on her father's behalf. It was a measure of
Christy's true naïveté that she didn't realize how laugh-
able her plan was. The down-home policewoman and
the nation's sexiest TV star, Laura thought wryly. Even
the supermarket tabloids would blink before printing
that particular headline.

She was, however, too wise to let on that she'd understood Christy's plans. "Of course I don't mind if you
go to bed," she said, smiling easily. "Have a good
night's rest, and I'm sure you'll knock 'em all dead
tomorrow, whichever outfit you choose."

"Maybe I could give you a call after I get home from
school and tell you how everything went?"

She sounded so hesitant, so uncertain of her welcome, that Laura found herself smiling encouragingly.
"That would be fine. Or perhaps you'd like to come
around to my apartment next Sunday. How about if I

cooked up some of my special hamburgers in exchange for tonight's super-deluxe pizza?"

Christy's eyes glowed with genuine pleasure. "I'd like that a lot," she said. "And so would Dad, I'm sure." She didn't give either of them a chance to respond to this suggestion, but walked over and gave her father a quick kiss on the cheek. "Good night, Dad. Come in and see me before you go to sleep?"

"I will. Sleep well, honeybun. And if you have nightmares, remember it's only your third slice of pizza talking."

Chapter Seven

THE SOUND OF Christy's footsteps had scarcely died away when Laura stood up and brushed a few pizza crumbs from her jeans. It was all too obvious, Ben thought, that she planned to leave immediately, if not slightly sooner. He had been watching her closely all evening, and he knew he would have a hard time persuading her to stay. But he had no choice, dammit. He had to keep her here until he could find some way to bribe or coerce her into closing Christy's official file. He had to find some way to stop her from calling Renee.

The problem was how. He could probably seduce her without too much difficulty, and the bedroom was often an excellent place for discovering a woman's vulnerabilities. Ben didn't think he was conceited in assuming he could sweet-talk Laura into his bed. He doubted his sexual technique was any more exciting than the next man's, but he would have been a fool not to recognize that his money and his Harrison Brand image combined to act as overwhelming aphrodisiacs for most women. Added to which, Laura might be streetwise in many ways, but he would guess he was a hundred times more experienced in bedroom games than she was. Surely it wouldn't be difficult to keep her sexually infatuated long enough for his lawyers to get to work.

And yet, oddly enough, he was reluctant to turn on the slick Harrison Brand charm. Laura was so open, so transparently honest. Once already this evening he'd almost risked everything and told her the truth. But that was a dangerous strategy. Too damn dangerous to risk again. She might be kindhearted and honest, Ben reminded himself, but she was also a veteran police officer.

And the police department had to be kept cut of things. Aaron was working his tail off, filing legal motions and working out a cash settlement that was enticing enough to keep Renee permanently away from Christy. But until those motions were accepted by the court, Ben couldn't afford to have Laura talking to his ex-wife. He was breaking the law, and he'd deliberately set out to trick a police officer.

Ben felt himself break out in a cold sweat. Dear God, he'd been careless to assume Laura would consider the case closed once she'd seen those out-of-date custody documents. He'd recognized how conscientious she was, how attentive to detail, and yet he'd made no efforts to prevent her from returning to work. He'd actually been anxious to get rid of her, not liking the strange, uncomfortable emotions she provoked in him. A mere fluke had kept Cristy safe. Thank heaven Renee always registered at hotels under her lover's name. He shuddered to contemplate what would have happened if Laura had managed to speak to his ex-wife.

If Renee found out where Christy was staying, she'd whisk the poor kid away immediately—then haul him into court so fast that he wouldn't even have time to pack a toothbrush. What's more, she'd undoubtedly take the greatest delight in seeing him thrown into jail, at least until her tame lawyer explained that convicts don't make much in the way of money.

Money always spoke a great deal louder than anything else as far as Renee was concerned. That was what these last four years of hiding Christy had been all about. In retrospect, Ben realized he'd been an absolute fool to threaten Renee with loss of her child-support payments unless she shaped up as a mother. She'd treated his threats all too seriously and immediately taken steps to ensure that he could never put them into effect. And the person who'd suffered most had been Christy—the only person entirely innocent in his and Renee's screwed-up relationship.

Which all brought him right back to the point where he'd started. He had to keep Laura here, and be damned to this uncomfortable feeling that she deserved better than to be treated to his standard seduction routine.

"Thanks for a great pizza," Laura said, breaking into his skittering, angry thoughts. She held out her hand, smiling the friendly, slightly shy smile that always stirred an odd, half-forgotten tenderness somewhere deep inside him.

"But you can't go yet," he protested, taking her hand into both of his and clasping it lightly. Deep down inside he already knew what he was going to do, but a small part of him stood back, appalled at the cynicism of his actions. Remember Christy's happiness is at stake, he reminded himself, putting his arm around Laura's waist.

He gazed down at her with every ounce of Harrison Brand charm that he could muster. "Don't go, Laura, the night's hardly begun. Keep me company for a while, please?"

The shy smile came and went again, almost before he could register it. "Ben, I appreciate your courtesy, but you don't have to play the polite host just because Christy's put us in an awkward situation. We both know she's at an age where she lets her enthusiasms run away with her."

He was surprised at how easy it was to return her smile. Dammit, he really *did* want her to stay, and not just because of Christy. "I'm not just being polite. With the kind of schedule I've had lately, I sometimes think I've forgotten how to be polite even when I want to be. Please stay, Laura. I very much want to find out more about you."

She planned to refuse, he knew it, but she hesitated just long enough for him to sit down and pull her gently onto the sofa next to him. Close to him, but not too close. He didn't want her to feel nervous. This was one seduction scene that couldn't be rushed to its inevitable conclusion.

"You see how painless that was," he said, smiling. He made sure it was a warm, friendly smile, with no sexual undertones. As he'd expected, some of the tension slowly left her body.

"Now, can I trust you to stay put?" he asked, pitching his voice carefully, making it low-key and faintly teasing. "I'd like to fix us both an after-dinner drink. Any special preferences?"

"I'm not much of a connoisseur. Usually all I drink is white wine and the occasional beer."

That was pretty much what he'd expected. "I'll find you something appealing," he said, concealing his satisfaction. Not brandy, he thought. Something sweet, so she won't register the alcohol as she drinks it down. It wasn't that he planned to get her drunk, he assured himself. Just relaxed enough to let down some of her guards. He strolled over to the bar and tipped crushed ice into two crystal goblets, then added an almost lethal dose of Cointreau.

He carried the drinks back to the sofa, handed one to

her, and raised his glass in a lighthearted toast. "Here's to fatherhood. Let's hope the good Lord grants me the energy to survive next week."

She looked amused. "I think you'll need to survive a bit longer than a week if you want to see Christy through the traumas of adolescence."

"Yes, but I'm smart enough not to intimidate myself." She laughed and he grinned back at her, sliding his arm casually along the back of the sofa. Laura, intent on sipping her Cointreau, gave no sign that she'd noticed his move. So far so good.

"All right," he said. "Time to get down to the nitty-gritty of the biography of Laura Forbes. You have to tell me the three most important things that have happened to you since your twentieth birthday."

She shook her head in mock protest. "Ben, I already told you my entire life history when we were sitting on the side of the mountain."

"Nonsense. All you told me was that you're from Iowa and your boyfriend ran off with your college roommate two days before the wedding."

Her brown eyes laughed up at him. "Ben, that *is* my entire life history. Remember, I come from four generations of God-fearing Iowa farmers. My folks believe that if you're doing something that can't be written up in the family Bible, then you shouldn't be doing it."

She looked so pretty—not beautiful, just entrancingly pretty—that for a moment he forgot why he was setting out to seduce her. He put down his glass and reached out unthinkingly to touch the tendril of hair that started to curl forward onto her forehead. A delicate wave of pink colored her cheeks, and he experienced another of those aggravating surges of tenderness. Good grief, what was the matter with him? Surely he ought to be past the stage of finding himself turned on by semi-virgins.

With single-minded ruthlessness, he pushed the tenderness away. For his daughter's sake he needed to discover this woman's vulnerabilities, not waste time exploring his own. I only need a week, he thought. Ten days maximum if Aaron does his job properly. Besides, is it so bad if I try to seduce her? Dammit all, she's an adult and a free agent. She can always say no.

He drew his forefinger across her mouth with cool calculation, feeling the faint quiver of her lips beneath his touch. If he kissed her now, he didn't think she would resist, but he drew back just in case. Better if he waited until she was a little bit hungrier for his touch.

"I've never been to Iowa," he said, leaning back with every appearance of total relaxation. "Please tell me about it."

She sat ramrod straight on the edge of the sofa, clearly ill at ease with his proximity. "About three million people live there," she said, taking another small, neat sip of Cointreau. The sweet, orange-flavored liqueur obviously appealed to her. "The main industries are all connected with agriculture. Iowa was the birthplace of Herbert Hoover and Buffalo Bill Cody, and there's a famous prehistoric Indian burial site at Marquette—"

"No," he interrupted softly. "That's not what I meant. Tell me about *your* Iowa."

She looked away from him, rattling the melting ice cubes against the side of her glass, and for a moment he thought she was going to remain silent. "We live on a farm way out in the country," she said at last. "The water comes from wells and we generate our own electricity. My mother looks like she stepped out of a Norman Rockwell painting, and my brothers look ten years older than they are because they've worked so hard for so many years."

"Are your brothers married?"

"Very much so. My sisters-in-law are dedicated

homemakers who think women only become feminists if they can't catch a man."

He glanced at her, genuinely intrigued. "Don't you find that rather annoying?"

"Sometimes, but they're so warm and loving, it's hard to resent them. They worry about me because here I am, nearly twenty-eight years old, no obvious flaws or defects, and still without a man. I've tried to explain that it's much better to be single than married to the wrong person, but they don't think that's much of an excuse. According to them, no man is ever good husband material until a woman's had a chance to work him over and pummel him into shape. Every so often, I point out that I'm hoping to marry a man, not the Pillsbury Dough Boy, but they both feel I'm making excuses."

He laughed. "I think you're more patient than I would be. How many nieces and nephews do you have?"

"No nieces, but four extremely tall and skinny nephews, whose main characteristic seems to be that they eat."

"Soul mates to Christy," Ben murmured.

"Oh, no!" She laughed fondly. "Christy's a finicky eater in comparison to my nephews. Between them, they can get through two loaves of bread just for a mid-afternoon snack. When you walk into the kitchen back home, it always smells wonderful because Mom bakes every day. She does that in between caring for her vegetable garden, raising a milk cow, tending two goats, and supervising a flock of chickens. She dries all our laundry out of doors, except when the temperature's below freezing, and when you go to bed the linens smell of grass and prairie wind. We eat outside a lot in summer. Hamburgers, corn on the cob, potatoes baked on the grill." She stopped abruptly, her eyes very bright. "Well, anyway, you get the picture."

"Yes, but I want you to tell me more." To his surprise, he wasn't lying. The images she conjured up provoked an almost hypnotic appeal. "I'm an only child and I grew up in the middle of New York City, so I can't imagine what it would be like to be part of a big family, living on a farm. How did you entertain yourselves? Did you have neighbors within walking distance?"

"Just one set, the Johansens. Russ's family. He was one of five boys."

"Russ?"

"My former fiancé. You remember, the one I was engaged to for nearly four years before he ran away to marry my best friend."

"Oh," he said with mock solemnity. *"That* Russ. The one with no taste in women."

She laughed ruefully. "Ben, you've never seen how gorgeous my roommate was. Believe me, Russ had excellent taste."

He took her glass of Cointreau and held it to her lips. "Drink up and drown your sorrows," he instructed. "Who knows? Maybe she'll be fat and flabby before she's forty."

"Wonderful thought, but haven't you noticed life is rarely that fair?" The laughter suddenly faded from her eyes, leaving them bleak and curiously leached of color. She put her glass down on the coffee table and stared blindly into its depths. "No," she whispered. "When you get right down to it, life usually isn't very fair."

"Laura, what is it? What's wrong, honey, please tell me." He took her hands in an instinctive gesture of comfort, holding them tightly within his own. They felt very cold.

She turned slowly toward him, although he was sure she didn't see him because her eyes were misted over with tears. "My brothers are losing the farm," she blurted out. "They took out a second mortgage to pay for new machinery and to build a cottage for my brother

Jim's family, and now the bank's calling the loan. By the end of the month the farm won't be ours anymore. They're going to lose everything."

Tears rolled silently down her cheeks and he took her into his arms, patting her back in the same sort of soothing gesture he might have used on his daughter. "Are you sure?" he asked. "Can't they sell off the machinery? Or work out some sort of extended-payment scheme?"

"They've tried everything," she said, her voice muffled against his chest. "The problem is the bank's in trouble and nobody wants the bank to go under. There have been too many bank failures this year already, so the directors have called in every loan over thirty thousand dollars. No exceptions and no excuses, even though our farm will show a slight profit when the summer crops are sold."

"How about a federal loan? Didn't Congress recently vote in a few hundred million dollars of extra farm aid?"

"Yes, but my brothers aren't eligible, unfortunately."

"I'm sorry, Laura," he said, wishing he could think of something more adequate to say. "Truly sorry. You must feel as if you're being torn up by the roots."

"It's not so bad for me. After all, I left the farm when I went away to college and I've never been back except for vacations. It's my family that I worry about. The farm isn't only their livelihood, Ben. It's their whole lives."

He cupped her face in his hands, brushing away the tears with his thumbs and stroking her cheeks softly, comfortingly. He searched to find the right words to take away some of her hurt. "Sometimes we find that people are more resilient than we'd ever expected. It may not be as bad as you think. Your whole family sounds like survivors to me."

"I hope so. Oh, Ben, I do hope you're right." She pulled away from him, apologizing with considerable embarrassment when she realized that her tears had soaked the front of his shirt.

"Hey, that's okay. What else were broad masculine chests invented for, if not to cry on?"

She smiled, albeit a touch tremulously. "Thanks, Ben," she said simply, then sniffed, a valiant, inelegant sniff that had the strange effect of making his heart feel as if it were melting. He realized suddenly that he wanted to kiss her, that in fact he'd been wanting to kiss her again ever since those moments they'd spent by the waterfall.

He continued to stroke his hand against her cheek, but there was no longer anything comforting in his gesture. He brushed his forefinger across her mouth, the movement deft and deliberately erotic. Her lips parted on a tiny sigh and he bent his head toward her mouth, insinuating one hand into the soft tangle of her curls. With casual expertise his other hand glided down the smooth satin of her blouse until it curved around the swell of her breast, his practiced fingers automatically seeking out one of her nipples and teasing it into a state of urgent arousal. She made a little sound of pleasure deep in her throat, and he felt the instant, throbbing response of his body. He was shocked by his own reaction. It had been a long time since he found such simple foreplay so arousing.

He could imagine just how good she was going to taste when he finally kissed her, but he was used to employing skillful techniques to heighten his partner's enjoyment, so he kept their lips fractionally apart, tormenting them both with the prospect of pleasure. He was unprepared when she suddenly stirred in his arms, tilting up her head and joining her mouth to his with naive, unsophisticated eagerness.

Something tight and hot exploded inside him, sending fire coursing through his veins. He could no longer stand back and calculate the effect of his moves. He kissed her hungrily, greedily, thrusting his tongue into her mouth, craving her response. When her hands clutched at his back, he felt himself shudder. She provoked in him a need he had almost forgotten, a need for unity with another human being, for the merging of more than abstract parts of their bodies.

The need was strong enough and painful enough to make him angry. His mouth ground down against hers, rough as well as demanding, and he was almost relieved when he felt the spark of fear in her, the tiny movement of withdrawal. Renee had taught him the risks of confusing emotion with sexual pleasure, and he'd learned his lessons well. He might plan to seduce Laura to suit his own purposes, but he sure as hell didn't want to start feeling anything toward her other than mild liking, or admiration for her well-kept body. The brief moment of stark sexual hunger she had produced in him was as dangerous as it was inexplicable.

Ben drew away, his breathing ragged, fighting against the crazy impulse to take her into his arms and pull off her clothes so that he could rain hot, open-mouthed kisses all over her body. He wished she would toss off some witty, sophisticated comment that would put the whole damn episode into proper perspective. But of course she didn't. She was too blasted naive to pretend an indifference she didn't feel. She curled against the pillows of the sofa, her hands hugged modestly around her waist, but her eyes still dazed with passion and her lips soft, swollen, and faintly bruised.

"Laura, honey, I'm really sorry. I didn't mean to come on so strong." Ben felt only mild surprise when he heard himself apologize. Laura seemed to provoke so many unlikely reactions in him that one more hardly seemed worth bothering about.

Her face was already flushed from their lovemaking. He watched, fascinated, as her skin darkened to a deep shade of pink. "Don't apologize," she said huskily. "I liked what we were doing. It felt . . . wonderful." She turned away, pressing her hands to her flaming cheeks. "Oh, heavens, please forget I said that. It must be the alcohol talking."

For her perhaps, but not for him. Two beers and a few sips of Cointreau weren't enough to explain away his actions over the past few minutes. And twice that amount of alcohol wouldn't explain why he was reaching out to her again, pulling her back into his arms when he ought to have been running as fast as he could in the opposite direction. Their mouths met urgently, tongue seeking tongue without any preliminary dalliance. His hands sought her breasts, but his usual expertise was entirely lacking. He pulled at the ties of her blouse, fumbling with the loose knot. He slid the soft satin from her shoulders, feeling his fingers shake as he reached behind her to unhook her bra.

Her body was as perfect as he'd known it would be, although until the instant he saw her naked, upthrusting breasts he hadn't realized how vividly she'd already stamped herself upon his imagination. In his routine seduction scene, now would be the moment to murmur sweet nothings, to tell her she was beautiful, to whisper between kisses how much he wanted her. But his mouth was too dry to shape the words. Instead, he kissed the pulse throbbing in the hollow of her throat at the same time that his hand moved slowly down toward the apex of her thighs. She moaned softly, her hips arching up into his palm at the same time her hands reached inside his shirt, splaying against the hot skin of his back.

Their clothes suddenly seemed intolerable barriers, condemning them to lonely, frustrating isolation. He wished they were already naked, her skin slick against his, her heart pounding, her nails digging into his spine as their bodies moved to become one. Simultaneously he realized that he had to slow the headlong pace of their lovemaking, or they would end up taking each other half-clothed on the living room sofa. For himself, right at this moment, the idea had definite appeal, but for Laura's sake, he wanted to make their first time together a little more romantic. He was surprised, in fact, at how much he wanted it to be something she would remember with unshadowed pleasure. Reluctantly he tore his mouth away from their kiss and carefully held his body a few inches away from her until he regained control of his breathing.

"Darling," he murmured, allowing himself the tantalizing satisfaction of nuzzling her ear. "I think it might be better if we continued this in my bedroom."

For a split second he thought the strangled gasp he heard came from Laura. Then the gasp was repeated, louder and more insistent, and he realized it came from the doorway. He looked up swiftly, retaining just enough presence of mind to keep Laura pinned down among the sofa cushions, where she was more or less obscured from sight.

A third muffled gasp, this time from much closer at hand, was followed by an outpouring of incoherent apologies from Prudence Datscher, his secretary. He scarcely bothered to listen to what she was saying. His attention was fixed on the couple framed in the doorway. Renee, his ex-wife, and the barracuda in human clothing who passed for her lawyer. Eric, that was his name. Eric Ashburton.

Ben rose slowly to his feet, blessing his training as an actor, which enabled him to keep his face virtually expressionless. He looked covertly at Renee, reflecting that the past four years had been kind to her. At thirty-five, she appeared several years younger and her face was as cute and dimpled as ever. He'd always thought it amazing that such a greedy, cruel woman could look so cherubic. Renee, he'd learned to his expense, was living proof that faces didn't always reflect their owners' character.

Out of the corner of his eye he could see Laura searching among the sofa cushions for her blouse. Her face was pale and her lips trembled, and he felt a flare of fierce anger that she was being subjected to this humiliation.

"Well, what a surprise for all of us," he drawled, positioning himself so that Laura was effectively screened by his body. Hearing rustling sounds as she put on her blouse, he deliberately drew attention away from her by unfastening his zipper and casually tucking his shirt back into his pants.

Renee, of course, was not so easily distracted. "Oh, my Lord, Eric," she fluttered, clutching her hand to her heart in a gesture that would have done Mary Pickford proud. "Heavens above, I do declare we've walked in on an orgy! And my poor little baby daughter right here in the house!"

Sickened, Ben turned from Renee's grandstanding to look at his secretary. "Would you mind telling me, Prudence, just how these two people got into my house?"

Prudence had the grace to look embarrassed. "I was coming back from a concert at Boettcher Hall and they drew up in the driveway in front of me. Of course I recognized Mrs. Logan—I mean the former Mrs. Logan—and so I thought you'd want me to let them in." She tilted her chin with a touch of guilty defiance. "I had no way of knowing what was going on in here. I mean, the door wasn't even shut."

Ben looked at his secretary in deadly silence, and the self-righteous flush faded from her cheeks, leaving her pale and gaunt-looking. "I'm sorry," she whispered. "Ben, I'm truly sorry."

He controlled his temper. No way would he give Renee and her tame shark the pleasure of seeing him angry. "I understand why you did it," Ben said quietly. "Good night, Prudence. I'll see you tomorrow morning."

Prudence turned abruptly, but Ben saw the tears gathering in her eyes even before she reached the hallway. What a god-awful mess, he thought wearily, and he was the person most to blame. In retrospect, his selfishness seemed unforgivable. He'd known for months that his secretary was falling in love with him and he'd avoided tackling the problem simply because Prudence was so good at her job. He'd spotted the unmistakable signs of jealousy and resentment when he spent time with his daughter over the past few days, but he'd simply ignored them, hoping his secretary would come to terms with her own emotions. Now he was paying the price for his insensitivity.

Glancing around he saw that Laura had managed to put on her blouse and do a quick repair job on her hair. Inevitably, she still look faintly disheveled, but she got to her feet with an innate dignity that he couldn't help admiring. He held out his hand, silently drawing her to his side. She felt soft and yet strong against his body.

Renee, never one to appreciate being out of the limelight, apparently decided she'd been quiet long enough. She cast a quick glance in Laura's direction, taking in the tousled hair and the still-swollen lips, and for a single unguarded moment her expression became ferocious. Then she swayed delicately. "Oh, Eric," she moaned, "let me lean on your arm, or I swear I'm going to faint! I just can't bear to think of my little baby in this house of sin!"

"Christy is asleep in her room, getting plenty of rest before she starts school tomorrow," Ben said curtly. "Please cut the histrionics, Renee. There's nobody here to appreciate them."

Her china-blue eyes flashed with malice. "Histrionics? You call concern for my poor little girl histrionics? I came to your house to rescue my precious baby and found you conducting an orgy with some floozie—"

Ben felt Laura stiffen, and he shoved his hands into his pockets so he could resist the temptation of grabbing Renee by the shoulders and shaking her until her teeth rattled. With the greatest difficulty he managed to keep his voice sounding calm and faintly bored. "I'd be careful what accusations you fling around, Renee, if I were you. Maybe a few introductions are in order. This is Laura Forbes, a very good friend of mine. Laura, as you've probably guessed, this is Christy's mother, Renee Baruch"—Ben stressed Renee's maiden name—"and her . . . companion . . . Eric Ashburton."

Eric smiled, showing a great many orthodontically perfect teeth. "Well, now, Mr. Logan, I think we should strive for a little more accuracy here. I'm Ms. Baruch's lawyer, not her companion, and we've flown all the way from New York City on a piece of very urgent business concerning the welfare of my client's young daughter."

"We've come to rescue my poor Christy!" Renee exclaimed, obviously tired of the lawyer's long-winded explanations. "The merest chance saved my little girl from your wicked clutches. We switched on the television news this morning and there she was—with you, in Vail!" She fumbled in her purse and quickly extracted a lace handkerchief—no doubt put there expressly for this purpose, Ben reflected cynically—and dabbed it to her bone-dry eyes. "I can't bear to think of it. My sweet daughter, snatched from my arms—"

"Christy wasn't snatched from anybody's arms," Laura snapped. "The truth is, Ms. Baruch, she ran away from your house and hitchhiked all the way from California to Colorado while you were vacationing in New York with your *lawyer*. You should be grateful she found her way here to Ben's house, or she could have gotten herself into a heap of trouble. Nasty trouble."

Renee temporarily at a loss for words, contented herself with glaring venomously at Laura and fanning herself with her handkerchief. The lawyer, however, was made of sterner stuff and launched into an immediate, unctuous monologue.

"I can't imagine why dear Christy should choose to deceive her mother, and I certainly can't begin to think why she would run to her daddy, the last person in the world who's capable of giving her the attention she needs." His mouth stretched into a wider and even more vicious smile. "Perhaps you don't know, Miss Forbes, that my client has had the sad duty over the past few years of explaining to her little girl that her daddy is such an unfit guardian that the judge absolutely forbade any contact between the two of them."

Ben's stomach twisted tight with a potent mixture of anger and fear. He turned to Laura just in time to see her startled gaze fly up to meet his. "That's not true, is it?" she asked. "You and Renee have joint custody rights, don't you, Ben?"

"Doesn't he wish," Renee's voice cut in malevolently. She looked from Laura to Ben, her eyes flashing dislike and barely suppressed triumph. "He's been trying to get back custody of his precious daughter for the last four years, and now he hasn't got a hope in hell." Somewhat belatedly she recalled her pose of wounded Southern womanhood and clasped her hands demurely in front of her. "Imagine," she said, fluttering her eyelashes in Eric's direction. "My darling baby girl brought back to this house, and it's just like it was before! Sexual license and misconduct right in the living room!" She smiled at Ben, her voice purring with satisfaction. "Well, Ben, darling, what do you think Judge Wendell will think of *that* when he hears it?"

"Too true, too true." Eric sighed with patently false regret, not giving Ben time to say anything. "Yes, my dear Renee, I fear it's our sad duty to report to the judge that your former husband's morals haven't improved one bit in the past few years. Tragic that poor little Christy should be deprived of contact with her daddy, but I'm afraid no judge could change his custody decision when he hears our account of what was going on in this house. Poor Renee! You'll just have to struggle on alone, as you've been doing these past four wearisome years. I daresay Judge Wendell will order Mr. Logan to make higher support payments to Christy now that she's getting older and her expenses are so much greater."

"Yes," Renee commented. "An increase in my child-support allowançe would probably help to ease the terrible hardship of raising my baby girl alone."

Ben swallowed hard, fighting a wave of nausea. A dozen conflicting thoughts rushed through his mind, but paramount among them was a fierce determination not to allow his daughter to fall back into Renee's mercenary and unloving clutches. He was still holding Laura's hand, so he felt the tiny movement she gave and knew she was going to speak. Without any conscious fore-knowledge of what he was going to do, he put his arm around her shoulders and turned her toward him, holding her against him in a deliberately intimate embrace.

Her gaze, wary and a little hostile, flew up to meet his. If he'd had any room inside him for concerns other than Christy's well-being, he might have felt guilty over the way he planned to use her. As it was, he could think of nothing but the overriding need to save his daughter. He cupped Laura's face in his hands, preventing her from speaking as he leaned over to whisper in her ear. "Please help me, Laura. For godsake, don't let them take Christy."

Keeping his arm lightly around her shoulders, he lifted his head just enough for Renee and Eric to get a good view of his adoring expression. "Darling," he murmured huskily, gazing earnestly into Laura's eyes, "I really think we'll have to tell them."

"T-tell them?"

"Yes, darling, I'm afraid so, although I know you wanted to keep it a secret and avoid all that wretched publicity." He turned smoothly to face the lawyer. "Before you start making all sorts of threats about my daughter and accusations about orgies in the living room, I think you should know that Laura and I are about to be married. And I'm sure Judge Wendell, just like any other judge, will think she's an excellent stepmother for Christy." He paused for a calculated moment, then added, "Laura's a police officer."

Renee dropped her lace handkerchief, and Eric's smiling teeth momentarily disappeared from view. To Ben's enormous relief, Laura had apparently been rendered speechless, for she simply continued to gaze up at him with enormous eyes, making no effort to deny his outrageous statement.

Neither Renee nor Eric was speechless for long. They broke into a joint tirade that, in other circumstances, Ben might have found funny. Eventually, wearying of their abuse, he cut into their diatribe.

"Okay, Renee, I've heard it all before. Just tell me how much it's going to cost to get you and your sidekick out of here. Without Christy, of course."

The lawyer recoiled in exaggerated horror. "Mr. Logan, surely you're not suggesting that my dear client and I would set a price upon her little daughter's moral well-being!"

"That's exactly what I'm suggesting, Eric. Are we going to keep up this charade any longer, or do you want to discuss terms?"

"Mr. Logan, Mr. Logan, you grieve me with that sort of talk. Let me remind you that you're in no position to cast aspersions on anybody else's motives. Remember that Christy is here in your house illegally. My advice to you is to wake your daughter up right away and hand her over to my dear client, so that we can take her to our hotel for the night."

"Over my dead body," Ben said with lethal calm. "Name your price, Eric, or I'll get Juan to throw you out and to hell with whatever lawsuits you decide to bring."

Renee didn't give her lawyer a chance to speak. "Ten thousand," she said curtly. "Then Eric and I will leave."

Ben's lip curled faintly. "Ten thousand it is." He strode over to the escritoire and opened a small, locked drawer. He extracted a checkbook, scrawled out a check, and handed it to the lawyer. "Good night," he said curtly. "If you call my lawyer in New York, he'll suggest a permanent financial deal that you and Renee might find interesting."

"I want cash up front," Renee said. She flicked the check Eric was holding. "And don't get any fancy ideas about stopping payment on this, or we'll be back here with a whole damn troop of lawyers, and the police, too, for that matter." The word *police* seemed to set off a whole new train of thought, for she jerked her head around and subjected Laura to a sudden, intense scrutiny. When she looked back at Ben, her gaze was speculative.

"I don't believe you have any intention of marrying that rinky-dink cop. She's nothing like the sort of woman you're usually attracted to."

"That's true," Laura said coolly. "But Ben's taste in women has improved quite a bit over the past fifteen years."

Ben actually felt himself smile. Good for you, Laura, he thought proudly. Don't let the barracudas put you down.

He returned to Laura's side, taking her into his arms with an exaggerated display of loving possession. He kissed her on the forehead and then, more lingeringly, on the lips. "Don't go away," he murmured throatily. "I'll just see our visitors to the front door, and then we can take up where we left off."

Eric pocketed the check, his expression disgruntled. "No need to see us out. We know the way."

Ben's smile flashed cruelly. "I think I'd prefer to see you off the premises. Laura and I will rest a little easier once we're certain that you're gone."

Renee's lips tightened into a thin line. "You'll be hearing from us, Ben. Don't think you've bought us off with a measly ten thousand dollars."

"My dear, I never dreamed for a minute that you could be bought so cheaply. I know an expensive whore when I see one."

The sound of her hand slapping against his face echoed along the hallway. Still the same old Renee, Ben thought. Nothing had ever enraged her as much as the truth.

Chapter Eight

BY THE TIME Ben returned Laura was shaking with a potent mixture of rage and several other less easily identifiable emotions. As soon as he set foot in the living room, her temper exploded. For some reason it was easier to shout at him than to sit quietly and explore what she was really feeling.

"What have you come back for?" she yelled, totally ignoring the fact that it was his house. "Are you going to *escort* me off the premises, too, or do you want to take a longer look at a first-rate patsy? Good grief, you must think I'm greener than Iowa grass."

"Laura, let me explain." He reached out to take her hands, but she jerked them away, the anger still flowing hot and molten within her.

"Explain what? You've been lying to me ever since we met. Not just casually, but systematically, with malice aforethought."

"Not with malice," he said quietly. "Believe me, Laura, never that."

118

"Huh! So how would *you* describe what you've been doing? What fancy Hollywood term would you come up with to describe your behavior? You set out to deceive me from the moment I asked for proof of your right to custody. Presumably those documents your lawyer sent were all fakes—"

"Not fakes exactly. Just a few years out of date."

"That amounts to the same thing, as you darn well know. You tricked me into leaving Christy in your care when you didn't have a legal right in the world to keep her. And in the process you put my job on the line. Not that my job would seem in the least bit significant to somebody like you, I guess. My ambition to make detective must seem pretty small potatoes to somebody who's shooting for a paycheck of a million dollars an episode."

"Seventy thousand an episode," he corrected wryly, running his hands through his hair. "Of course your job seems significant to me, Laura. For heaven's sake, my insensitivity hasn't yet reached the point where I believe people's salaries are the only measure of how much they're worth. I'm sorry for the way I tricked you, more sorry than I can say, but did you really expect me to turn Christy back over to her mother? Good God, woman, you saw what Renee was like! Vampires could take lessons in bloodsucking from her."

Laura had indeed seen, which was why she'd made no effort to stop Ben from negotiating the illegal deal to keep his daughter. The fact that she'd consciously broken the law tonight didn't make her feel one bit better. She whirled around angrily, still not even trying to bring her temper under control.

"Whatever Renee may be like, she happens to be Christy's legal guardian, and you, apparently, have been barred even from visitation rights. Judges don't decide to keep a father away from his child without cause.

Judge Wendell must have had good reasons for rescinding the original custody arrangement."

"He did. Excellent reasons. Renee set me up."

"How? Judges aren't easy to deceive."

His mouth twisted bitterly. "No judge would be a match for Renee and Eric when there's money at stake. She was very clever. We had problems with the custody arrangement right from the start. I was constantly denied access to Christy and eventually the situation degenerated to the point where Aaron advised me to go back to court. Then, out of the blue one day, I got a phone call from Renee. She sounded amazingly reasonable, asking me to meet her alone at a friend's place in Connecticut. To talk things over informally, she said. Like a total fool, I agreed."

"Why was that foolish?"

"Because I should have known Renee better. God knows, after nine years of marriage I should have known the sort of things she was capable of doing. When I arrived at the house, you could hardly see through the marijuana smoke in the hallway. That alone should have been enough to warn me, but instead of turning tail and running like hell, I was dumb enough to walk in and start asking for Renee. A lot of very helpful people immediately directed me into a small bedroom where one almost naked girl was lying on a bed and two others were waiting right inside the door. They grabbed me by the arms and led me over to the bed. I got as far as saying 'Where's Renee?' when the door burst open and a horde of policemen ran in. I think maybe they arrived a few seconds earlier than they were expected, because I still had all my clothes on, although the girls had managed to unfasten quite a few of my shirt buttons. You're a cop, so you can guess the rest. Aaron barely saved me from being arrested on vice and drug charges. And by the time Renee and her lawyers got through with recounting the incident to Judge Wendell, it sounded as if awarding me custody of Christy would be tantamount to selling the child into white slavery." Ben's mouth tightened into a hard, cynical line. "Believe me, a similar situation would never arise again. In the past four years, I've learned to be a little smarter and a lot more devious."

Laura felt her anger begin to dissipate in a rush of sympathy, but she forced herself not to show what she was feeling. Her emotions tonight had already experienced all the thrills and spills of a giant roller coaster ride, and she was very aware that she was capable of doing things she might later regret. Dangerous things. Like going into Ben's arms and holding him close. Like reaching up and pulling his mouth down to hers so that they could shut out their problems in a storm of passionate lovemaking. Like telling him that she . . .

But that was too dangerous even to think. Laura quickly fanned the fading embers of her anger. Anger, right now, seemed a relatively safe emotion. "If you were set up as you claimed, you ought to be able to get Judge Wendell's decision overturned."

"I've been trying for four years," he said wearily, his skin stretched taut over suddenly prominent cheekbones. "But when you play in a series like *Empire* and have paparazzi from the gossip magazines making every innocent dinner date sound like the preliminary to an orgy, it isn't easy to win your case. I've had one appeal turned down already."

"I'm sorry," she said sincerely, forgetting to be angry. "Can't your lawyers get you another hearing?"

"They've gotten one," he said, and the weariness of his features hardened into ruthless determination. He closed the small gap between them, putting his hands on her shoulders and forcing her to look up at him. "Renee and I have another custody hearing scheduled for the middle of next month, and this time I plan to win."

"I hope you do. Christy—"

"I absolutely can't afford to have Eric drag any more pseudoscandals under Judge Wendell's nose," Ben interrupted. "That's why I claimed you and I were engaged and about to be married. I'm sorry to have involved you in this mess, Laura, but I want you to know I'm deeply grateful for what you did tonight. By keeping silent, you saved Christy from being shipped back to live with two people who don't love her at all."

Laura's lungs suddenly seemed too small for her breath to squeeze through. So here it was. They'd finally reached the subject she'd been trying not to think about. Of course, she'd known all along why Ben claimed to be engaged to her. Even though she hadn't been thinking very clearly once they started making love, she'd retained sufficient command of her wits to understand why he'd made such an outrageous statement. Naturally, she'd understood all along that none of those whispered endearments were real. Nevertheless, the memory of Ben holding her close while Renee and Eric looked on still had the power to make her feel . . . embarrassed. Yes, Laura decided, the emotion she felt right at this moment was almost certainly embarrassment.

She cleared her throat and clasped her hands neatly in front of her. For some reason it was important that she look and sound businesslike. "Yes, well that's another thing, Ben. The little show we put on tonight may have bought you a few hours time, but have you considered what's going to happen when your court hearing comes up and Eric discovers you're still single? Surely he's going to make a big issue out of the fact that you lied to him."

Ben looked at her speculatively. "I was rather hoping Eric wouldn't discover I was still single."

She frowned, genuinely puzzled. "Aren't you underestimating your opponent, Ben? Beneath all those hideous fake smiles and phony Southern idioms, Eric struck me as a shrewd lawyer. Surely a man of his resources would have no difficulty turning up evidence that you never remarried?"

"That would depend."

"Ben, all he has to do is demand in court that you produce your wedding certificate."

"With your help, I could produce one."

She stiffened. "Are you suggesting I help you to prepare a fraudulent certificate? Quite apart from—"

"Of course I wasn't suggesting forgery," he interrupted calmly. "As a matter of fact, I was suggesting we might be able to produce the genuine article. An honest-to-goodness Colorado marriage license."

Laura's heart began to beat very fast. She clasped her arms tightly around her waist to hide her shaking hands. "Sorry, but you're not making too much sense, Ben."

"It's simple. I want you to marry me as soon as we can arrange a ceremony. By the end of next week at the latest, sooner if possible. It's the perfect solution to our problems."

She was sure she turned white. She knew, beyond question, that she was shaking. *"Our* problems?" she asked with freezing coldness. She needed to speak coldly because for one reckless instant she'd found herself thinking how wonderful it would be to accept his proposal!

"Yes, *our* problems. You need money in a big hurry. I need a wife in an equally big hurry. If my time with Renee hadn't left me so darn paranoid about the whole institution of marriage, I'd have realized years ago that a respectable stepmother for Christy was the perfect solution to my problems. And, like I said to Eric, I can't think of a more respectable stepmother than a police officer with loads of experience in dealing with juveniles. Judge Wendell will be tickled pink."

The wild racing of her pulses was caused by distaste for Ben's crazy proposition, Laura assured herself, not insidious delight at the prospect of being married to him. She had to refuse him now, quickly, before she was tempted to ask him what he meant about the money. Could he possibly have meant . . . No, she mustn't even think about how much he might have been prepared to pay her. She didn't need any further temptation.

She drew herself up very straight and managed a reasonably cool smile. "It's an interesting suggestion, Ben, but I don't think it would work out too well in practice."

"Why not?"

"Because marriage is tough enough when two people are in love. It must be totally impossible when they don't even know each other."

His eyes gleamed in wry acknowledgment. "I'm not suggesting we commit ourselves to a lifetime of togetherness, Laura. I'm talking about a short-term, strictly practical arrangement that would benefit both of us."

She wouldn't waste time asking herself why his words were like knives dragging across her skin. "I think you've been reading too many of *Empire*'s rejected scripts, Ben. Marrying a virtual stranger to obtain custody of your daughter strikes me as a dangerous case of overkill. Pretty much on a par with chopping off your head to cure a migraine."

He grinned. "You can't deny that would effect a dramatic cure."

"Dramatic certainly. But most people are smart enough to prefer a pill and a darkened room, even if it takes a while longer for the pain to go away."

His expression sobered. "Laura, let's stop beating around the bush. I need your help and I'm prepared to pay for what I need. What would you say to thirty thousand dollars up front and a bonus payment when we split up, say a thousand dollars for every month we've been together? I could ask Aaron to draw up a prenuptial contract that was fair to both of us. You must know some reputable lawyer who'd look it over for you —"

"Thirty thousand dollars!" She scarcely realized that she'd interrupted him. "Ben, did you say thirty thousand dollars?"

He looked at her shrewdly. "Yes," he said. "Up front. Enough to stop the bank foreclosing on your family farm, Laura."

She could save the farm! Her mother wouldn't have to live in a poky apartment and her brothers wouldn't have to work in a hardware store when their hearts yearned for the land. Thirty thousand dollars! She couldn't understand why she didn't leap at the chance to save her family. Surely she would have been crying with happiness if her throat hadn't been choked with tension and some other emotion that left her hurting too much for tears.

"It would be an excellent arrangement for both of us," Ben persisted softly. "Not to mention how great it would be for Christy. You have some idea of what she's been through these past few years. It's a miracle she's limited her rebellion to coloring her hair purple and running away. If the judge sends her back to Renee, you know better than I do what will happen." He took her hands, folding them into the warmth of his clasp. "Laura, please say yes. This is a situation where everybody wins. Everybody involved gets what they want. Your family, my daughter—"

"And me?" she said tightly. "What do I get, Ben?"

"Financial security," he replied promptly. "The chance to pursue your career if that's what you want. The chance to be a homemaker if you'd like that experience for a couple of years. The knowledge that you're making a lot of other people extraordinarily happy."

Laura looked down at his hand holding hers so confidently. "Ben, you're making something totally crazy sound . . . commonplace, ordinary. But it isn't ordinary at all. There's more to marriage than applying for a license and moving your clothes to a different closet."

He grinned. "Hell, Laura, a man doesn't agree to change his closet without giving the matter a great deal of serious thought."

"You know that isn't what I meant."

"Then tell me what's bothering you," he said. "The forced intimacy? Instant motherhood? Sex?"

"All of it," she mumbled miserably. Never since her first bewildering days away from the farm had she felt so tongue-tied, so totally unsophisticated. "I just don't know, Ben."

He cupped her face in his hands and kissed her lightly on her lips. "Let's take care of your problems one by one. I have two homes, so we can be as intimate or as distant as you choose. You'll be a terrific mother, we both know that. As for the sex, well . . ."

He leaned down and sealed her mouth with a kiss that started off gently persuasive and ended up hotly passionate. When they finally broke apart, Ben spoke quietly. "I don't know what you think, but somehow I doubt we're going to have any problems in that direction."

"Just because something feels good it doesn't mean it's right," she snapped.

"Ouch! I hear four generations of stern Iowa farmers talking."

"Ben, this is never going to work. I can't cut myself off from the past, from the way I was brought up."

"You don't have to," he said. "Laura, I can find sex almost everywhere I look. Somebody like you, a mother for Christy, is virtually unique. If you think we might have a good time together in bed, that's great. If you prefer to keep our relationship strictly platonic, that's equally okay with me."

Laura wondered whether she should laugh, cry—or throw something hard and heavy straight at his patronizingly smiling face. She turned her back on him, hugging her arms into her stomach. She understood, at last, why she was so reluctant to accept his proposal. Ben was offering her a marriage of convenience, with a little companionship and sex on the side if they both happened to feel the urge. But she didn't want that sort of marriage. She, poor fool, was already more than half in love with him. It was scary to think just how far past the halfway mark she'd already traveled.

For a minute or so she paced the room, pretending to consider his proposal. In reality she knew her answer was a foregone conclusion. As Ben claimed, their marriage would provide simple solutions to several problems, and she could hardly pretend that living with him would require major sacrifices on her part. Of principles, perhaps, but certainly not of pleasure. Living with Bennett Logan, in fact, was likely to prove perilously enjoyable.

She swung around and regarded him silently, noting the stubble beginning to darken his cheeks and the crow's feet fanning out from around his eyes. See, she reassured herself, he's losing his mystique already. A few weeks of living in the same house, and I'll wonder what I ever saw in him.

She ignored the tightening of her stomach muscles and swallowed. Hard. "All right," she said, proud that her voice sounded so controlled. "I agree. We'll be married before the end of next week."

She saw relief—and something else—flare momentarily in the depths of his eyes. Then he was smiling with a cool civility that matched her own. "Let's shake on it," he said, extending his hand. "I'm sure we'll both find this a very satisfactory arrangement."

Laura clasped his hand with the briskness the situation seemed to demand. "I'm sure we will," she said. "By the way, I would prefer to continue working. That way I'll have a career to go back to when . . . when we arrange the divorce."

"Of course, I agree that seems best. Unfortunately,

the shooting schedule for *Empire* means that I'll need to commute between Denver and L.A. for a good bit of the year, but with you here, I know Christy will get all the stability she needs."

"It would certainly be better for her to go to school in one place," Laura agreed politely.

"Then I guess we have nothing left to discuss apart from the date of the wedding," Ben said. His manner would have been entirely appropriate if he'd been arranging a time to have his hair cut, or maybe some slightly less enjoyable appointment, like a rendezvous with his dentist.

Laura wasn't to be outdone. "The department's going to be shorthanded next week, so I don't want to ask for extra time off. I could be free next Wednesday, if that's a good day for you."

Ben walked over to the escritoire and consulted his calendar. "Wednesday looks great," he said. "That gives us a week before I have to fly back to L.A."

Gives us a week for what? Laura wondered. She didn't ask, of course. Instead she made a big show of picking up her purse from the sofa and jotting down a note in her pocket diary. As if she would be in danger of forgetting the date of her own wedding! She closed her purse with a defiant snap.

"It's two o'clock, Ben. I'd better be making tracks for home."

"Are you sure you wouldn't care to spend the night?"

She looked up quickly, but his expression was merely courteously inquiring. "Thanks," she said, "but I have to be at work by seven tomorrow morning."

With a splendid display of concern over having kept her up so late when she had to start work so early, Ben escorted her out to the driveway, where her Ford Pinto waited in solitary splendor. "Would you like me to drive you home?"

"I'm used to driving alone at night, thanks all the

same." She smiled a very small smile. "In case you've forgotten, I am a cop."

He opened her door and held out his hand once again. "Well, thanks for everything, Laura. I'll be in touch some time tomorrow."

"Leave a message on my answering machine if I'm not home," she said.

"Will do. Good night, Laura. Take care."

"You, too, Ben." She turned on the ignition and waved politely before maneuvering her car out of the elegantly curving driveway.

Her mind remained obligingly blank until she stopped at a traffic light and rested her forehead wearily against the steering wheel. Ben was wrong, she reflected with a cyncism that was new to her. He didn't always recognize an expensive whore when he saw one. It had cost him thirty thousand dollars to buy her off. Renee had cost him only ten. Whichever way you looked at it, twenty thousand dollars was a flattering premium. She hoped—desperately—that she wouldn't derive too much pleasure from earning her pay.

Chapter Nine

JUAN ARRIVED WITH the Mercedes promptly at noon on Wednesday. Laura opened the door and he immediately bowed low, handing her a posy of creamy-pink rosebuds with a flourish.

"From Mr. Logan," he said, eyeing her full-skirted silk dress with undisguised approval. "My boss, he has chosen very well. The flowers and the color of your dress, they are almost the same."

She took the flowers with a murmured word of thanks. Her hands, she noted with detachment, were perfectly steady. A slight compensation for the fact that her stomach was busy pretending to be a barrel tumbling in free flight over Niagara Falls.

"You are happy today, Miss Forbes, I can see it. Your complexion is like magnolia blossom in spring. No wonder Mr. Logan is so anxious for your arrival." Juan beamed, delighted with his elegant compliment. "If you give me the key to your apartment," he added more prosaically, "I will return this afternoon and move all

130

your belongings to Mr. Logan's house. You have packed your suitcases, yes?"

"Yes, they're all packed." Laura handed over the keys and followed Juan obediently down the stairs.

Fortunately they met none of her neighbors and she was able to sink into the welcome anonymity of the Mercedes without having to explain what in the world she was doing all dressed up in a fancy silk dress and matching high-heeled sandals.

In fact, she wasn't quite sure how she'd allowed herself to be persuaded into wearing such an obviously bridal outfit, except that Ben had kept insisting Christy would like her to wear something special. "And we'll have to take pictures for your family," he'd pointed out.

After three phone calls—she hadn't actually seen Ben in person since the night she agreed to marry him —Laura acknowledged the justice of his arguments. Her family would certainly expect to see lots of pictures filled with happy, smiling faces. Since smiles might end up in short supply, she might as well dress the part.

Laura glanced down at her watch. Only twelve-fifteen, but her whole family would already be lined up in the living room at the farm, slightly self-conscious in their best Sunday clothes. The bottle of champagne — perhaps even two since it was a *very* special occasion — would be on the table waiting for one o'clock when Laura had told them she would call to say the wedding was over.

The images were so vivid and so familiar they brought a lump to her throat. And yet, even the members of her family had revealed a few unexpected facets over the past few days. Her phone conversations with them hadn't gone quite as she'd expected.

Her brother David had been the first to hear that she was getting married. "You won your bet, Mom!" he called out, laughing.

Her mother picked up the phone. "I knew you were

serious about Ben," she said with smug satisfaction. "I told David you'd be marrying him before the summer was over, and I was right."

"But Mom, how could you possibly—"

"As soon as I heard you say his name, I knew he was somebody special."

"Mom, he's a TV star. I probably sounded impressed when I mentioned his name because it's kind of famous!"

"Laurie, honey, I'm old enough to recognize how a woman sounds when she's in love."

She started to protest. "But Mom, I was only joking when I told you—" She broke off, at a loss for words. What was she going to say, after all? That she'd only been trying to cheer them up when she joked about getting married? That she didn't love Ben in the least? Her brothers were proving sticky enough about taking the money, refusing to consider it anything other than a short-term loan. If they ever discovered the truth about her marriage to Ben, she would never persuade them to accept a penny. Maybe, in the long run, it was better if she allowed her family to maintain their romantic illusions. At least until she broke the news that she was getting a divorce.

She was glad when Juan interrupted the depressing train of her thoughts. Obviously considering the occasion too momentous for a discussion of baseball, he launched into an enthusiastic commentary on the preparations for the wedding. "Unfortunately, Prudence Datscher had to go back to L.A. three or four days ago. Urgent personal business, Mr. Logan told me. But everybody else will be there."

"Everybody?" she queried, nevertheless relieved to know that Prudence wasn't going to be hovering around, looking tall, glamorous, and subtly disapproving.

"The staff," Juan said hurriedly. "And Mr. Logan's

friend from New York, who is also his lawyer. The caterers have prepared a feast, Miss Forbes. You will be pleased."

Caterers? She couldn't imagine why they needed caterers. Of course they had to entertain the judge who would marry them, but she had imagined something simple like champagne and petits fours from a local bakery. Ben really seemed to be going overboard to convince Christy this marriage was for real. In some ways Laura was touched by this further evidence of his concern for his daughter. In other ways she wished the ceremony hadn't developed into something quite so elaborate. What with her expensive new dress, Juan's exuberance, and Ben's gift of roses, her fantasies were in danger of getting out of hand.

Once they arrived at Ben's house, Juan put his hand under her elbow and carefully escorted her up the front steps. Long before they could knock the door was swung open by a white-coated waiter. "Welcome, Miss Forbes, and best wishes from all the catering staff," he said, smiling. "The judge arrived ten minutes ago, so everybody's ready and waiting."

Even to Laura's bemused senses there seemed to be an unexpectedly loud hum of chatter bubbling from the living room. "Mr. Logan has prepared a little surprise for you," Juan said, his smile now stretching almost from ear to ear. "I think you will find some very important visitors flew into Denver last night."

He pushed open the door. "Here comes the bride!" Juan announced, clearly relishing his role as master of ceremonies.

The murmur of voices died away into silence as Laura paused on the threshold, overwhelmed by the sight that met her eyes. Most of the furniture had been cleared out of the room to make way for the cluster of people seated on neat rows of gilt-painted chairs: her mother; her brothers and their wives, and four gangly nephews, who all seemed to have grown a minimum of three inches since she'd last seen them.

For a moment she couldn't move or speak. Her family swiveled in their seats, smiling a welcome, but they didn't rush to hug her as they usually would have. Instead she had the impression they were all holding their breaths, waiting expectantly for what they knew would follow.

Laura walked slowly down the aisle between the rows of chairs. The glass patio doors had been decorated with an arrangement of cascading roses and baby's breath, and two men whom she didn't know stood to the left of the arch. Christy, dressed with surprising demureness in pale lavender voile, jiggled impatiently between them. Her purple hair seemed to vibrate with suppressed excitement.

Ben stood slightly apart from the others, looking strangely unfamiliar in a formal dark-gray suit and starched white shirt. Sunlight caught the gold of his hair, burnishing it with fire, but his blue eyes gleamed dark with shadows. Against her will she felt her gaze lock with his. Some indefinable emotion arced between them, and then, as she had feared, it was impossible to look away.

He came forward to meet her, taking her hands and raising them slowly to his lips. His mouth brushed against her knuckles, cool and yet oddly reassuring. Laura heard her family let out a collective sigh. So that was what they'd been waiting for, she thought abstractedly. They'd wanted to see how Ben would greet his bride.

He continued to hold her hands, the posy of pink rosebuds clasped between them. "You're so beautiful you take my breath away," he said, his voice husky.

She looked up at him, wishing he wasn't such an accomplished actor. Was there any chance that he really did find her beautiful? she wondered. Her heart squeezed tight with a curious sensation somewhere between pain and ecstasy. "Thank you for the flowers," she said, not knowing what else to say.

He leaned forward, placing a fleeting kiss on her forehead. "My pleasure. Come and meet Judge Ritter, who's going to marry us, and Aaron Schrenk, who volunteered to brave the wilds of Colorado to act as my best man."

The judge looked more like a good-natured leprechaun than a sober member of the legal profession. Aaron, on the other hand, could have been dispatched by Central Casting to play the part of a distinguished lawyer. Laura smiled as she shook his hand.

"I hope you survive your exile to the wilderness. As long as you keep to the highways, you'll probably be safe from wild bears and marauding Indians."

He laughed, his gaze openly admiring. "It's looking less of a wilderness by the minute," he said. "Trust Ben to requisition the prettiest woman in the state before I can get here and demonstrate my superior charms."

"Don't you bring any of your city slicker wiles out here," Ben admonished with mock seriousness. He lifted Laura's hand to his mouth, pressing a kiss into her palm and curling her fingers around the kiss. "This pretty lady is definitely mine."

"Not quite yet," Judge Ritter interjected amiably. "But it might be a good idea to start the ceremony before you two 'best friends' come to blows."

Ten minutes later, the wedding ceremony was over. "By the authority vested in me by the state of Colorado, I now pronounce you husband and wife." The judge's eyes twinkled. "You may kiss the bride, Ben, and then it's my turn."

Laura's brothers gave an uninhibited roar of approval as Ben swept her into his arms and proceeded to kiss her with unmistakable thoroughness. The formalities over, her family descended upon the newlyweds in a mass of loving hugs and excited questions. Her sisters-in-law welcomed her into the sorority of married women with beaming approval. As far as they were concerned, little Laurie had finally taken the first step toward fulfilling her destiny as a woman.

Her mother, sporting a jaunty yellow hat with artificial daisies around the brim, made no attempt to hide the tears streaming down her cheeks.

"Thank you for arranging to get us here," she said to Ben. "It means more than you can imagine to see Laura looking so happy."

"I have a daughter of my own," Ben replied. "I think I know how you feel, Mrs. Forbes."

"My friends call me Barbara," she said, accepting the champagne offered by a passing waiter. "And you sure do qualify as one of our friends." She raised her glass. "Here's to you and Laura. Love and good wishes from all of us for a long and successful marriage." She smiled mischievously. "From the little bit I've seen of you so far, Ben, looks like you almost deserve to have won our Laurie."

"Mother!" Laura exclaimed, feeling her cheeks flame, but Ben only laughed. "Hey, Christy, get over here quickly! I need moral support from our side of the family. Will you please tell your new step-grandmother what a terrific person I am?"

"I already did," Christy said. "This morning over breakfast. I tried real hard to be convincing."

Everybody laughed, and Laura took the opportunity to give Christy a hug. "Your outfit is so cute," she said softly. "Especially the lace stockings. Thanks for being such an efficient bridesmaid."

"I only had to hold your flowers while Dad put on your ring." Christy bent to examine the delicately chased gold band. "Do you like it?" she asked shyly. "Dad and I chose it together."

"I think it's perfect," Laura replied truthfully.

A waiter glided to her side. "Canapes, ma'am?"

"No, thank you," she said, softening her refusal with a smile. "I guess I'm too excited to eat."

"I'm not," Christy remarked ruefully. "In fact, I'm starving."

Laura laughed. "In that case I suggest we look around for my nephews. Wherever they're standing, I guarantee we'll find food."

Glancing around the room, she spotted the boys in a far corner, clustered around a small table. Sure enough, when they reached the corner, they found the table piled high with sandwiches, cookies, chocolate cupcakes— and an untouched platter of fresh fruit.

"Hi, guys," she said, embarrassing them all by planting a firm kiss on each of their cheeks. "Have you met my new daughter . . ." The word was so strange on her tongue that for a moment she stumbled, then she quickly recovered herself. "My new daughter, Christy Logan. Christy, in descending order of size, this is Danny, Matt, Ken, and Steven Forbes."

"We already met last night," Christy said, acknowledging the introduction with a definite gleam of appreciation in her eye.

Amused, but a little startled, Laura looked again at her "little nephews" and realized that, from a teenage girl's point of view, they had a lot to recommend them. Danny and Matt were not only tall but decidedly well muscled about the arms and shoulders. Even the younger Ken and Steven had somehow avoided the usual plague of adolescent pimples, and their clear gray eyes stared at Christy out of attractively tanned faces.

"So what's good to eat?" Christy asked, leaning casually against the table.

Four eager voices immediately extolled the merits of everything on the table, except the fruit. Laura laughed, making her way back toward the center of the room.

"Watch out, or you might accidentally eat something that's good for you," she commented.

Ben came up to her and seized her hand, pulling her into his arms. "Your whole family's watching us," he whispered, pretending to nuzzle her ear. "Let's make this a good one, shall we?"

Before she could protest, his hand curved around her waist and his fingers splayed across her spine, pressing her curves into the hardness of his body. Laura's heart began to hammer against her ribs, and she closed her eyes, shutting out reality. She ought not to let this happen, she thought, not in a crowded room with all her family watching. They were not the sort of people to approve of public demonstrations of affection. Even though nobody was likely to guess Ben's lovemaking was all for show, she ought to resist; her pride was at stake, if nothing else.

"Don't, Ben," she murmured.

"Don't stop?" he queried laughingly, his breath already caressing her lips. "All right, honey, I promise not to stop."

His mouth touched hers, light and warm and subtly demanding. It was humiliating to feel the way her body immediately melted. It was heaven to feel the increasing urgency of his embrace.

Heaven won out, with scarcely a struggle. Laura stopped fighting the irresistible and gave herself up to the pleasures of Ben's kiss.

The sun had vanished behind a bank of late-afternoon clouds when Ben and Laura arrived at the Brown Palace Hotel in downtown Denver.

"Looks as if there's a thunderstorm brewing," Ben commented as they waited for their room key.

"Yes, it's a good thing we didn't have far to drive."

"With your family staying in Denver for such a short time, I thought you'd prefer to spend the night in town.

That way you can visit with them tomorrow morning before their plane leaves."

"I'd certainly enjoy that."

Silence descended, a distinctly uncomfortable silence. Laura racked her brains feverishly. Surely there must be something witty and/or mildly amusing she could say to the man she'd just married. The trouble was, everything she wanted to say seemed embarrassing or provocative. Or worse.

She could always comment on the impressive galleried design of the lobby, unchanged since the hotel was built at the end of the nineteenth century. But somehow she couldn't help feeling she ought to be able to come up with a more intimate topic of conversation than pioneer architecture.

Fortunately one of the assistant managers returned at that moment with their key. "Here you are, sir. The suite is on the twelfth floor and the bellboy's already taken your luggage. If there's anything at all we can do to ensure your comfort—"

"Thank you," Ben cut in. "I'm sure everything will be to our satisfaction."

The assistant manager looked down at the registration slip. "Mr. and Mrs. Richard Johnson," he murmured, then smiled hesitantly. "Has anybody ever told you that you look amazingly like that actor who plays Harrison Brand on television? You know, the man on *Empire* who just got parachuted into some Middle Eastern country?"

Laura held her breath, but Ben merely laughed resignedly. "Oh, yes, it happens all the time. In fact, you wouldn't believe how often I've signed paper napkins and old *TV Guides* because people kept insisting I had to be Bennett Logan. Frankly, I don't see the similarity myself."

"Oh, I don't know, dear," Laura interjected, overcome by a sudden imp of mischief. "I've always told you that your nose is just like Bennett Logan's. And your hair's *almost* the same color. Even my mother says so."

The assistant manager and Ben exchanged man-to-man glances. "Well, people believe what they want to believe," Ben said indulgently. "I keep telling my wife that if she ever got to see Harrison Brand without all the makeup they plaster over his face, she'd realize we don't look a bit alike. The man probably doesn't have a muscle in his body that isn't silicone injected."

"Too true," the manager agreed. "We've had a few movie stars staying here in our time and as far as I'm concerned, they hardly ever live up to their reputations. Well, enjoy your stay, Mr. Johnson. You, too, Mrs. Johnson."

Ben was openly laughing by the time they reached the elevators. "I can see I'm going to have to teach you some proper respect 'Mrs. Johnson.' Let me tell you that this nose of mine has more character than an upstart like Harrison Brand could begin to handle."

"He might surprise you, dear. Think of all the silicone he pumps into his muscles."

Laura's laughter faded as they entered their suite. A small sitting room, tastefully furnished with antique reproductions, led into a large bedroom, dominated by a quilt-covered, king-sized bed and a large, luxuriously equipped bathroom. Their two small overnight bags already sat on special stands at the end of the bed, left there by the bellboy. Laura gulped. This was it, she thought despairingly. The awful beginnings of physical intimacy without any mental intimacy to go along with it.

Ben seemed to share none of her tension. He threw himself onto the bed and bounced gently. "Nice and firm," he remarked casually. "I hate a bed that's too soft, don't you?"

If he was going to be so darn nonchalant, then she'd

be nonchalant, too. Even if it killed her. "I'm one of those lucky people who can fall asleep anywhere," she said.

Ben slipped off his jacket, unfastened a couple of shirt buttons, and began to loosen his tie. Laura swallowed hard. Dear God, he surely wasn't expecting them to . . . Not now. Not while it was still daylight.

He got off the bed and slung his jacket over his shoulder, picking up his small suitcase en route to the closet. Laura forced back a totally irrational feeling of disappointment. What in the world was the matter with her? She'd spent the best part of the past week telling herself that this marriage to Ben would only work if it was kept strictly platonic. She ought to be thrilled to bits that he seemed so totally unmoved by the bizarre intimacy of their situation.

She perched miserably on the end of the bed and watched as he unpacked a pair of slacks, a sports coat, and a couple of clean shirts, humming beneath his breath as he moved between the closet and the chest of drawers. It was all too obvious that sharing a hotel bedroom was no novelty to him. She was beginning to wonder how any newlywed couple ever managed to consummate their marriage. It was one thing for two people to get swept away by passion; it was quite another to sit on the end of the bed and try to work out the least embarrassing way for two strangers to transform themselves into lovers.

Ben had finished his unpacking. "Would you like to use the bathroom first?" he asked politely. "I think we should have dinner reasonably early, don't you? The waiters kept passing by me with trays of food, but I never seemed to eat anything."

"Nor me. An early dinner sounds great," she said, wondering how she would ever manage to ingest food over the lump of nervous tension lodged square in the middle of her throat. "I'll take a shower and change into something more comfortable. If we have time, that is."

His blue eyes watched her with quiet amusement. "We have all night," he said. "Remember, we're a married couple now."

As if there were any way she could forget.

Chapter Ten

LAURA ACCEPTED THE waiter's offer of a second cup of coffee, but she knew dinner couldn't be stretched out much longer. The moment when they would have to re-enter their suite and face that giant, king-sized bed was looming closer by the second.

Ben had already finished his brandy and was staring reflectively into the depths of his glass. Almost for the first time since Judge Ritter had pronounced them husband and wife, Laura was aware of a slight aura of tension emanating from Ben.

She wondered at the cause. It couldn't be nerves or self-consciousness, that she was sure of. Moving in the circles he did, he must have taken so many women to bed that he would long since have overcome any inhibitions.

She had a sinking suspicion that he was not looking forward to the chore ahead of him. She didn't doubt that Ben genuinely wanted her as a stepmother for Christy, but that, of course, didn't mean he also wanted her in his bed. Surrounded as he invariably was by beautiful and sophisticated women, Laura couldn't believe he really felt any strong attraction toward her. More than likely she simply provoked a vague feeling of sympathy, what with her all-too-obvious naïveté and even more obvious state of infatuation.

She looked up, and so did Ben. Their eyes met and Laura felt something soft and yearning begin to unfurl inside her. At that moment she finally allowed herself to acknowledge the truth. She wanted Ben to make love to her. Whatever his reasons, even if it was only because he felt sorry for her, she wanted—desperately—to know the ultimate fulfillment of his lovemaking. She pushed her coffee cup away, suddenly unable to bear the thought of another sip.

Ben watched her thoughtfully. "Tired?" he asked.

"A little bit."

"So am I." He shrugged ruefully. "I guess getting married will do it to you every time." He gestured toward a distant waiter who materialized with amazing promptness at their side. Even under the ordinary name of Mr. Johnson, Ben still exuded the sort of innate magnetism that commanded prompt attention from headwaiters. "I'd like to sign the check, please."

"Yes, sir. I have it all ready."

Ben signed the check, and they rode in silence up to the suite, each using their supposed fatigue as an excuse to lean in separate corners of the elevator.

Their sitting room contained a small bar with a ready-stocked, miniature fridge. Ben poured two glasses of mineral water while Laura drew back the heavy draperies and pretended to be fascinated by the view of narrow city streets and buildings under construction. This section of the Brown Palace, she reflected, certainly didn't include scenic splendors among its many merits.

Ben carried the glasses over to where she was standing, leaning beside her and sharing the uninspiring view. He was scrupulously careful, Laura noted, not to touch any part of her body.

"We didn't have much time to talk during the past week," he said abruptly. "But I did quite a lot of thinking about our situation. How about you?"

"Truthfully, I was almost too busy to think."

"I was afraid of that. The fact is, I realized several days ago that I'd pressured you into accepting a deal in which most of the benefits are on my side."

Her head jerked up in genuine surprise. "Ben, you paid me thirty thousand dollars. I think most people would think I've done very well by our deal."

"Money is easy to give when you have a lot of it," he said simply. "You, on the other hand, are giving me two years or more of your life. And time is irreplaceable."

She smiled, touched by his serious expression. "It's not exactly a major sacrifice, Ben. As I understood the deal, you're not planning to haul me off to Siberia to live in a tent. You're not asking me to weave my own clothes or eat only fried seaweed. Surviving Christy's first boyfriend is about the worst thing that's likely to happen to us during the next couple of years."

"That sounds traumatic enough to make up for all the rest," he replied, only half-joking. He ran a hand through his hair and set his glass on the window ledge with a decided thump.

"Dammit, Laura, this is turning out to be a hell of a lot more difficult to say than I thought it would be. The thing is, I think our . . . arrangement . . . would be more comfortable for both of us if we keep it strictly platonic. I'm sure you must feel that way, too."

Her throat was suddenly so dry that she could only manage to produce a single word. "Why?"

"Why?" He seemed startled that she had questioned him. "Well, I guess there are a couple of reasons. Right now we have a pretty good relationship. I like and respect you and I hope, when you get to know me better, you'll feel the same way about me. Sex between us would complicate everything. Emotions would start to get in the way of what ought to be practical decisions. The whole beauty of our relationship is that it's strictly practical. You need money and I need respectability, so we've made an even exchange. Once we started throwing sex into the deal, who knows if we could preserve the balance."

"That's a new twist on an old theme." Laura was suddenly too hurt and angry to be cautious. "There can't be many women who learn on their wedding night that they've been bought strictly for their respectability. A mighty odd reason to buy a woman, don't you think?"

"Laura, I was thinking of *you*. God knows, if you'd like us to make love, it would be my pleasure to oblige you."

"To *oblige* me! For heaven's sake don't do me any favors."

He grabbed her as she whirled past him. "Hell, Laura, I've made a total mess of this whole conversation. I'm sorry." He drew in a deep breath. "Let me start over. You're a very desirable woman, Laura, and I would enjoy making love to you if that's what you want. If that's what you think is right for you."

She glanced pointedly at her captured wrist and smiled with deadly sweetness when he released her. "Don't even think of it, Ben. I wouldn't want you to put yourself to any trouble on my behalf." She picked up her glass, then quickly put it down again before she succumbed to temptation and flung it straight at the wall. Or him. "Good night, Ben. I think I'm going to take another shower. I feel as if I need one."

He watched her leave the room. "Hell," he said to his glass of water. "Hell and damnation."

* * *

When it was your third shower of the day, you could only make it last so long before you turned into a prune. With a regretful sigh, Laura switched off the water and wrapped herself in one of the hotel's thick white towels. She walked over to the sink and brushed her teeth, eyeing the peacock-green silk nightgown she'd hung on the back of the bathroom door. Even drooping from the hook, the gown had obvious flair, and the saleswoman had insisted it would prove totally irresistible. "So much more subtle than red or black, and perfect for your complexion, miss. You're lucky to have such wonderful skin."

Laura rinsed off the toothpaste. Wonderful skin, huh. Ben certainly didn't seem to have noticed it. She tossed the towel over the shower rail and cautiously dabbed Opium onto her wrists and the hollows of her throat. Having spent most of her life smelling of nothing more exotic than lemon shampoo and baby powder, even a small amount of such sophisticated perfume made her feel nerve-rackingly decadent.

That was the trouble, she reflected disconsolately, sniffing her arms. At heart she was a lemon-shampoo sort of person, whereas Ben had spent his adult life surrounded by what you might call French-perfume women. From his perspective, making love to an everyday woman like Laura must seem about as exciting as contemplating a lifetime of steamed-rice dinners.

Shrugging resignedly, Laura reached for her nightgown. The silk slid down her skin with a sensuous rustle, and she smoothed it over her body so that the thin, semitransparent fabric clung to the swell of her hips and the curve of her breasts.

She stared into the mirror, lifting her chin defiantly. Darn it all, she *did* have a good figure, if only Ben would take the time to look at it. And although she might not have much practical experience of how to make love, her dreams these past couple of weeks had certainly provided her with a dazzling array of theoretical possibilities. If she didn't lose her nerve, maybe Ben would find his plain rice dinner more stimulating than he'd ever expected.

She flung open the bathroom door—and was met with darkness. Not sure whether to take this as a good sign, she followed the glow of a faint nightlight and crept toward the bed. Sure enough, Ben was already there. Not only was he there, however; by all the evidence he was fast asleep.

Laura clamped down on a gasp of pained laughter. Silently, taking care not to disturb her brand-new husband, she crept between the starched white sheets and fluffy beige blankets. To her surprise, she realized after about five minutes that she was shivering, although the room was warm and there was no logical reason for her to feel chilled.

It was only when tears began to trickle out from under her eyelids that she allowed herself to acknowledge the truth. She was cold and crying because she hurt all over from Ben's rejection. Despite her best efforts, she had fallen in love with him and had spent the past few days dreaming that their marriage would eventually turn into a real and lasting union. She'd never accepted the idea of divorce after a couple of years.

Face it, she told herself, rolling over onto her stomach, you even considered getting pregnant without telling Ben. You saw how much he loves Christy and you hoped a baby would give him a reason to stick with the marriage. Why else did you arrive at this hotel without a single birth control device tucked anywhere in your luggage?

Loving him as she did, the fact that he'd fallen asleep during the brief time she spent in the bathroom was a devastating blow not just to her pride, but also to her heart. Not to mention, she thought wryly, the blow it had been to her hormones.

The Forbes family, however, was noted throughout Pocahontas County for its stubbornness in the face of overwhelming odds, and Laura decided during the course of a long, wakeful night that she had inherited more than her fair share of stubborn Forbes genes. She might not be able to turn this phony marriage into something honest and worthwhile, but she sure as heck was going to give it her very best try. She was a realist, and she accepted that she didn't have any of the qualities that would inspire Ben to love her, but she wasn't proud and she'd be willing to settle for second best: his acceptance, if not his love.

As for what she personally would get out of the relationship, she would have the pleasure of becoming Christy's mother; she would have Ben's companionship; and if he made love to her occasionally, surely that would be enough?

Laura ignored the sudden quiver of revulsion that coursed along her spine. After all, she decided, taking another shot at positive thinking, if she wanted Ben to make love to her, all she had to do was tell him. He'd already been kind enough to volunteer his services any time she felt the urge. In fact, she could scoot across the bed right now, tap him on the shoulder, and explain her predicament. *Excuse me, but I think I may go totally crazy if you don't take me in your arms and start making mad, passionate love.*

He'd probably respond with admirable expertise and typical Harrison Brand charm, but that wasn't the way she wanted their lovemaking to be. She wanted to make love to Ben, her husband, not to some stereotyped TV image of male sexuality. Most of all, she wanted him to come to her in passion, not out of duty or a misplaced sense of courtesy.

Quelling a hiccup of rueful laughter, Laura clasped

her hands behind her head and stared up at the ceiling. How in the world did she expect to inspire Ben to passion? What on earth did a medium-sized, brown-haired Denver policewoman have to stack up against the sensual sophistication of a TV star like Jill Cassell?

Laura devoted the best part of an hour to contemplating that problem. In the end, she concluded she had only two slight advantages over the luscious lovelies in Ben's usual entourage: he was her lawfully wedded husband, and they would be living in the same house.

For some reason that fragile hope was encouraging enough to send her to sleep just as the first pale rays of dawn light crept over the horizon.

By six-thirty in the morning, Ben could stand it no longer. He eased himself out of bed, having first drawn the sheet over Laura's shoulders so that he wouldn't have to look at the bewitching thrust of her nipples against the lace inserts of her nightgown. She seemed to have slept peacefully all night long, while he had scarcely managed to snatch more than a few minutes of restless dozing. Noble intentions, he mocked himself, sure were hell on a man's body. He ached from head to toe with frustration, and the worst of it was, he didn't even know why he was putting himself through all this. He'd bedded more women than he could remember, but now that he was finally married he was insisting on keeping his relations with his wife strictly platonic! That had to be one of his more screwed-up touches of chivalry.

He shaved and showered, wondering why Laura provoked such inconvenient protective urges in him. Why couldn't he just bed the woman and then forget about her? Lord knew, he'd done that often enough in the past few years. When his marriage to Renee ended, he swore his emotions would never again be held hostage by a woman. For five years he had found no good reason to alter that vow. Love, as far as he could see, brought only pain. Even his love for Christy had caused him years of anguish while he helplessly tried to find her.

Scowling into the bathroom mirror, he patted his face dry. A wise man knew he saved himself a lot of grief by not allowing himself to feel too deeply, and after everything Renee had put him through, Ben considered himself a *very* wise man. Laura was a cute kid, but she sure wasn't worth tying himself in knots over. No woman was worth that.

He came out of the bathroom and pulled on jeans and a casual, cotton-knit shirt. He dressed as quietly as he could, but some slight sound must have disturbed Laura. She stirred, turning in the giant bed. He stilled at once, but her head turned again on the pillow and her eyes flew open. She stared at him without expression for a moment, then she blushed.

He even found her blush sexy. Dammit, he wanted this woman in the worst possible way, but there was no reason to suppose he'd still want her once they'd made love. Why in blazes was he waiting? Why didn't he take her and get her out of his system? From the way she responded every time he kissed her, he couldn't imagine she would object to his lovemaking. He hesitated, on the brink of walking over to the bed and sweeping her into his arms.

She moved before he could take the first step, pushing herself up against the pillows, the sheet now carefully anchored to cover her breasts. "I'm sorry if I kept you waiting. Have I overslept?"

"Not at all. I happened to wake early this morning. It's barely seven o'clock."

His reply sounded curt, more curt than he'd intended because the feelings she evoked made him uncomfortable. Tenderness. Protectiveness. A desire for mental intimacy as well as physical closeness. He realized, with a touch of rueful self-awareness, that he was scared. Scared out of his mind. If he and Laura ever made love, he might not be able to walk away from the experience with a casual smile and a few graceful words of thanks. He was very much afraid that this shy woman with laughing eyes and minimum sexual experience would stir far more than his libido. And his emotions, he reminded himself, were strictly off limits. That was precisely why he needed to keep this relationship friendly and practical, just like he'd planned.

He gave her a big smile, one of his standard Harrison Brand charmers that paid no attention to the undercurrents of tension rippling around the room. "Your family's flight leaves around one. Would you like to go back to the house and eat brunch with them? There's no reason for us to hang around the hotel when you're probably longing to get back and talk to your folks."

"Thank you. Brunch with my family sounds like a great idea."

"Fortunately we'll be driving against rush hour traffic, so we shouldn't take more than twenty minutes to get home." He smiled, another beaming Harrison Brand special. If he didn't watch out, his jaws were going to crack. "I'm all through in the bathroom, by the way."

"Good." Without any warning she flung back the covers and yawned, stretching her arms high over her head. The peacock green silk of her nightgown tautened over the curve of her breasts, and her nipples—those damn nipples that had been haunting him all night long —thrust hard against the paler green lace insert.

Ben swallowed a groan. A man's noble intentions could carry him only so far. He fled, without speaking, for the sitting room.

The plane flying the Forbes family back to Iowa took off from Denver's Stapleton Airport almost an hour late, and by the time Laura and Ben arrived home in Cherry Hills, Christy had already returned from school. To

Laura's relief she and Ben were thus saved for an entire day from the embarrassment of having to find something meaningful to say to each other.

It was eight o'clock by the time they finished eating dinner, a delicious meal of chicken breasts Florentine and fresh strawberry mousse. Christy, thank heaven, had eaten with them.

"Coffee's in the living room," the housekeeper announced. "With whipped cream and Irish whiskey if you want to make your speciality, Mr. Logan."

"Thanks, Becky, you think of everything."

They trooped into the living room, and Christy, looking well pleased with herself, perched on the arm of the sofa. She had obviously misinterpreted the reason for the adults' unnatural quiet.

"Guess you two aren't in the mood for eating," she said, grinning. "I noticed neither of you had much dinner."

"It was delicious," Laura responded lamely. "Becky's a wonderful cook."

"She's only part time at the moment," Ben commented. "Would you like her to stay on full time?"

"It might be a good idea, since I work such erratic hours."

"I'll speak to her tomorrow." Ben poured steaming coffee into a fragile porcelain cup. "Would you like an Irish coffee? Becky seems to have gone to a fair amount of trouble whipping the cream and grating the nutmeg."

"Thanks, that would be pleasant."

Christy laughed. "There's no need for you two to be so gosh-darned polite to each other. We're *family* now."

Ben ruffled her hair. "Last I heard, there was no rule that people in the family had to be rude to each other. Here, Laura, I'll leave you to add your own sugar."

"Thanks, Ben."

Christy looked from one to the other, then yawned ostentatiously. "Well, I'm getting sleepy and I still have

loads of homework to do. Guess I'll go to my room."
She gave another cheeky grin. "Sure do hope you two
old fogies can dream up some way to entertain each
other once I remove myself." She blew an airy kiss in
each of their directions, then strolled out of the room,
leaving a frazzled silence behind her.

Laura sipped the hot Irish coffee and wished it was
neat whiskey, or maybe neat poison. In theory, she
should have been thrilled to find herself alone with Ben.
In practice, she was aware only of an overwhelming
shyness and a total ignorance as to what she should do
next. How did a woman set about seducing the man she
loved? Should she lean back against the sofa cushions
and cross her legs, displaying a tempting length of
thigh? But then, dreadful thought, maybe he wouldn't
find her thigh tempting. Or perhaps she should casually
unbutton her blouse? Except that it was hard to do anything casually when her fingers were shaking so much
that she could scarcely hold her coffee cup.

Her parents and brothers had taught her that nice
girls didn't make advances to men, and her experience
with her fiancé had reinforced his advice. Russ would
have been horrified if she'd usurped his masculine pre-
rogative and initiated any of their infrequent sexual en-
counters. Still, she was twenty-seven years old and
she'd assumed she'd overcome those inhibitions long
ago. This was a very inconvenient moment to discover
that six years of subscribing to *Ms*. magazine wasn't
enough to dispel nearly twenty-two earlier years of
hard-sell conditioning to meekness.

She watched, her heart in her eyes, as Ben carried his
coffee over to the corner of the room opposite the bar,
where a stereo system was built into the rows of book-
shelves. He fiddled with a few switches. "This is an odd
sort of question for a man to ask his wife, but do you
enjoy classical music?"

"Some, particularly the eighteenth-century stuff."

"Bach played on a laser disc system has to be heard to be believed. Do you like the Mass in B Minor?"

She loved it—at Easter-time, in church, but it was hardly lighthearted music by which to practice her wiles as a seducer. "How about something less serious?" she suggested. "A musical, maybe."

"Would you like to hear a new recording of *West Side Story?*"

"That would be terrific."

The energetic chords of the overture raced through the room. To Laura, the lively music merely emphasized the distance between them.

The music played on. Ben checked through his collection of discs, looking aloof, blasé, and very much Harrison Brand. Laura knew him well enough by now to realize he only adopted Harrison Brand's expression and mannerisms when he wanted to conceal what he was really feeling. What was he finding necessary to hide from her? Terminal boredom? Or some more flattering emotion?

"Did you ever see the movie of this?" she asked, desperate to break the silence between them.

"Not the movie, but the original stage show. My parents took me to see the production on Broadway when I was about twelve years old. I remember being totally stunned by the emotional power the actors generated. I came out after it was all over and informed my parents that I planned to be an actor when I grew up. My father wasn't amused."

"I'm surprised he took you seriously."

"My father was an unusual man. He tended to assume that if you said something you probably meant it, even if you were only twelve years old. Quite a refreshing attitude, when you come to think of it."

"Mmm, it is. What did your father do?"

"He was a family doctor, very much of the old school. My parents married late and I was an only child so there was always an unspoken assumption that I was going to follow in his footsteps. He had no particular objection to the theater for other people, but he certainly didn't expect his only child to waste his life in a frivolous profession like acting."

"Has he forgiven you now you're such a success?"

"Unfortunately he and my mother both died when I was still tossing pizza crusts and making the odd commercial, but we'd learned to understand each other pretty well long before then."

He walked back to the table in front of the sofa and put down his cup. "More coffee?"

"No, thanks."

They had now spent ten excruciating minutes exchanging chitchat and arrived back at precisely the point they'd started from. Coffee. Another success like that, and they'd soon find themselves discussing something really intimate, like the weather.

Laura returned her cup to the table and stood up. She and Ben were still a good four feet away from each other, but that was about three feet closer than they'd been the rest of the evening. She forced herself to look straight at him, but his eyes were shuttered, revealing nothing of what he was thinking. And yet she knew instinctively that he wasn't as unmoved or unaware as he appeared. Somewhere beneath those heavy-lidded eyes and cool smile, emotion was boiling.

She drew in a deep breath, her arms hanging stiffly at her sides. "Make love to me, Ben."

As an opening gambit, it made up in directness what it lacked in finesse. For a long moment he simply looked at her, and her breath quickened in response to the fire that leaped into his eyes. Then he turned away.

"Laura, I can't. It wouldn't be a smart move for either of us."

"Wouldn't it?" She walked slowly toward him, heat pulsing just beneath the surface of her skin. She'd gone too far now to turn back, and anyway, she was fairly sure he wanted her. Please God, he wanted her. But if she was wrong . . .

"Kiss me, Ben," she whispered.

He looked down at her, his eyes still heavy-lidded, but no longer inscrutable. Desire burned in them, naked and unconcealed, but he made no move to touch her. "Sex without commitment isn't for you, Laura. We both know it."

In his own way, she realized, Ben Logan was oddly honorable. He was warning her that he would take her if she provoked him any further, but he was promising her nothing beyond the physical union of their bodies.

She would have turned away from him if she could, but that option had died some time ago. Perhaps it had even died on the night she agreed to marry him. She reached out her hand and touched him very lightly on the lips, feeling a primitive flare of feminine triumph when his entire body shuddered in response.

He captured her hand and held it over his mouth, pressing a kiss into the palm. "I want you," he said harshly. "I want you like hell."

"I . . . I want you, too." Better, much better, not to embarrass them both by telling him what she really felt.

He said nothing more, simply sweeping her into his arms and carrying her toward the door.

"I promise to make it good for you, Laura. A night you'll remember."

He hadn't even kissed her, but she was already afraid he spoke only the truth.

Chapter Eleven

BEN FLIPPED A SWITCH as they entered his bedroom and a single lamp turned on, bathing the room in muffled, shadowy light. He carried Laura across to the bed and they sank together into the softness of the down comforter. She trembled, with excitement more than with fear, and he pulled her closer against his body so that she felt the hard thrust of his erection against the softness of her abdomen.

It was too late, too fierce, too immediate. Her fantasies had been more gentle. Desire and panic warred momentarily inside her, but he cupped her face and kissed her lightly on the forehead and her panic disappeared in a wave of love. She longed to touch him intimately, to slip her hands under his shirt and run her fingers over his arms and shoulders. But she was too shy. She wanted to caress the narrow line of hair that angled from his chest down to his stomach and beyond, but she was too inhibited. Oh God, she thought despairingly. What would happen if she could only lie on the bed, an unre-

158

sponsive lump of boring female flesh. Maybe Russ had been right. Maybe she was one of those women who melted when a man kissed her, then froze when he tried to progress any further. Maybe she was only a few steps away from being frigid. Why else had she spent the last five years being every man's best friend and nobody's lover?

At least Ben didn't expect her to be instantly ready for him. She could still feel the hardness of his body resting against hers, but his blue eyes were unexpectedly tender as he kissed her lightly on the lips.

"Don't look so uptight," he said, his fingers tracing the line of her cheekbones. "We have lots of time. All night if you need it."

"What about you?"

He grinned. "I'll take deep breaths and pride myself on my superb masculine control."

That was great for her, but it didn't sound very exciting for a man who had presumably made love to some of the world's most desirable women. "I hope this is going to work out," she said nervously. "The thing is, Ben . . . well, you've probably guessed that I'm not very experienced."

He dropped a casual kiss on the end of her nose. "All the better for my ego. You've only a few other men to compare me with. When it's all over, I'll lie back on the pillows looking self-satisfied, and you can tell me what a terrific lover I am."

She was silent too long, and he drew away from her. "Laura, you're not trying to tell me . . . Dear God, you're not a *virgin*, are you?"

He sounded so horrified that she actually smiled. "Don't worry, Ben, even if I were, it isn't catching. But as it happens, Russ and I were lovers." Or at least, she amended silently, we had sexual relations on a few less-than-memorable occasions.

"But are you telling me Russ was your only lover?"

"Well, yes." She turned away, embarrassed that in this day and age any woman could reach the ripe old age of twenty-seven with only one lover to her credit.

"Those Denver cops must be walking around with their eyes closed," Ben murmured. "Don't worry, Laura, this is going to be great for both of us."

He was being so darn nice, it was humiliating. Somewhat stiffly, she complied with his request that she should rest her head in the crook of his arm. How ridiculous this was, she thought. After nights of fantasizing about how she would flame into passion at Ben's first caress, here she was lying next to him with all the responsiveness of a sheet of plywood.

"I was seventeen the first time I made love," Ben said, his fingers weaving casually in the strands of her hair. "If a camera had happened to be around, I think it would have made a great disaster movie."

She laughed. "That bad, huh?"

"Or slightly worse. My unfortunate partner was probably the only person over the age of consent who knew less about what to do than I did. We kept bumping noses every time we tried to kiss."

She looked up at him, smiling, and he bent toward her, cupping her face as he brushed butterfly-soft kisses across her eyelids and the corners of her mouth. Warmth curled insidiously through her body, making her quiver.

"Your technique seems to have improved since then," she said breathlessly.

"Believe me, there was no way it could have gotten worse." He held her a little more closely and began to caress her back, sliding his hands down to her hips and up again to twine in the tumbled riot of her curls.

Laura let out a small sigh, relaxing against him. His exploration of her body gradually became more intimate, more demanding, but she no longer had any wish to call a halt. The slow, sure pressure of his hands was ecstasy. At last, she thought drowsily, at last she understood what sexual pleasure was all about.

Ben glanced down at her, smiling slightly. As if he had read her mind, he bent his head to kiss her, parting her lips with deep, slow strokes of his tongue that left her clinging to him, panting, shaking, and yet aching for more. Her drowsiness disappeared in a heated rush of desire, and her stomach slowly coiled itself into a knot of longing that was almost too intense to be pleasurable.

She couldn't hold back the moan forming deep in her throat when he slid her blouse from her shoulders. With a skill that might have depressed her if she'd still been capable of logical thought, he eased the transparent silk cups away from her breasts.

"You're even more beautiful than I remembered," he murmured, and her body arched up of its own accord as his mouth caressed the taut, sensitive nipples. His experienced hands found the zipper of her jeans and pushed the confining clothes away from her hips, then he pulled himself away from her just long enough to take off his clothes.

When they were both naked, he took her back into his arms, holding her close. The knot in her stomach tightened, sending out sparks of fire that raced along her veins until her skin turned hot and slick with desire. She was panting, but so was Ben, a sheen of sweat masking his forehead, and the muscles in his arms straining with the effort of holding back from the ultimate possession of her body.

"Ben . . . now," she whispered.

"Not yet," he murmured. "Trust me, darling, you're not quite there."

She wasn't sure where *there* might be, but if the feelings racking her body got any more intense, she was afraid she would disintegrate. She started to explain this to him, but her words died on a groan of pleasure as he slipped his fingers into the hot, moist darkness between her legs. She trembled at the wild, unrecognizable sensations his touch aroused, abandoning the last remnant of her inhibitions as she reached out to caress him in the same way he was caressing her.

At the first touch of her hand, Ben's breathing stopped, then raced forward again in shuddering gasps. Forgetting her shyness, forgetting that she really knew nothing about the technique of lovemaking, Laura leaned over him and kissed the hard, flat plane of his stomach. Then slowly, with deliberate provocativeness, she trailed her mouth along the path already forged by her hands.

His body jerked as though she had touched him with an electric current. After a few seconds he drew her back up onto the pillows, and his mouth quirked into a tiny, rueful grin. "Keep that up, honey, and this may be an unexpectedly brief encounter."

"Sounds good to me. Then we can start all over again."

He laughed softly. "Sweetheart, you've got to stop believing those publicity handouts. At my age, all-nighters are little more than a fond memory."

"I'll treat you gently," she whispered.

The laughter between them faded. His eyes darkened with unmistakable hunger and he cupped her face, taking her mouth in a sudden violent explosion of need. Without breaking the kiss, he rolled her over onto the pillows, pinioning her wrists high above her head as he suckled her breasts.

His tanned skin was rough against her smoothness, his body hard against her softness. The touch of his tongue against her nipples was total agony and pure, unadulterated joy. She twisted helplessly beneath his expert ministrations, her body writhing up to meet him as he finally moved into her, claiming her for his own. This, then, was what she had been waiting for—the exultation of being possessed by him, the vulnerability of giving herself into his possession.

With his mouth hungry on hers, with his body moving urgently inside her, there was no more room for fear, no more room for regrets. Love and passion flowed together inside her, racing each other to climax. She was reaching, searching, frantic, eager. She was soft, weightless, floating. The tension was unbearable, and she cried out his name, begging him for release.

His arms tightened reassuringly around her. "Yes, my darling," he murmured. *"Now* you're there."

She closed her eyes as he took her with him into ecstasy.

She was, after all, just another woman. Ben lay back against the pillows, taking care to avoid touching any part of Laura's sleeping body. His wife's body. He had known her less than two weeks. Odd how comfortably those words, *his wife,* reverberated inside his mind.

For some reason he was too restless to sleep, although he usually found sex an excellent nightcap. He got out of bed and walked across to the fridge in search of some chilled mineral water. He drank deeply, almost greedily, but the taste of Laura clung to his lips. The scent of her lingered on his skin, taunting him, tantalizing him with the knowledge that he still wanted her. Wanted her more, in fact, than before he'd taken her to bed.

But he wouldn't make love to her again, that was definite. Not unless she made all the moves. He tossed the cap from the mineral water into a wastepaper basket. A man could get addicted to Laura's softness, to her shy smiles, to the tiny incredulous flare of joy in her eyes the instant before she reached climax.

Ben slammed the fridge shut and walked back to the bed. Time for sleep. He had a busy day tomorrow.

There was certainly no good reason to turn and look at Laura.

On the other hand, there was no reason why he shouldn't look. Looking wasn't going to hurt anybody.

He rolled onto his side and propped himself up on one elbow. She was just a regular, ordinary woman, he reminded himself. A woman sleeping at this moment with the abandonment of total fulfillment. His heart gave a strange little lurch as he looked at her arm flung out on the pillows and her long, perfect legs coiled along the edge of the bed. A solitary brown curl had tumbled forward to cling damply to her forehead. He fought back an inexplicable urge to reach out and smooth it away from her eyes. There was no reason for him to touch her, no reason for him to touch his wife.

On the other hand, he could touch her if he wanted to. Why not? She was sleeping too deeply to be disturbed.

He would touch her on the waist or on the arm, nowhere very sensitive. And maybe that way he'd dispel this crazy impression that her body was more supple, more alive, more loving, than any woman's he had ever known.

He touched her hand. She didn't stir. That was what he had wanted, of course. He didn't want to wake her. Did he?

As if viewing the actions of a total stranger, he watched his fingers stroke slowly up Laura's arm and across her breasts. Her nipples hardened even before she opened her eyes.

She looked at him sleepily, not speaking, but her lips parted on a tiny sigh of pleasure and color tinged her cheeks. Looking down at her, Ben saw a woman waking to passion, utterly trusting—and totally vulnerable. Emotion, painful and unidentifiable, tightened his throat. Wordlessly he gathered her into his arms, burying his face in the lemon-scented fragrance of her hair.

Her body felt slight, almost fragile against him, and the tenderness he so much dreaded swept over him again.

"I shouldn't have woken you."

"I'm glad you did."

"Was it good for you—last time?" He was surprised at how much he cared what her answer might be.

She smiled, touching him lightly on the cheek. "It was perfect."

"No," he said, bending his head toward her lips. "Last time was good. *This* time it's going to be perfect."

By the end of her first week of marriage Laura had already passed through all the stages of simple neurosis and had moved well into the zone of the certifiably crazy. She decided that her relationship with Ben was designed to encourage schizophrenia. By night, the two of them were passionate lovers. By day, they almost never met and rarely spoke unless Christy was in the room to act as a buffer.

In fact, the only time Ben had spoken to Laura privately was on Monday morning, shortly after he received a phone call from his lawyer in New York.

"Aaron has good news," he said, beckoning her into his study as she was leaving for work. "Renee's lawyer has been in touch with him, and they're willing to work out a deal. Renee will drop all claim to custody in exchange for a guaranteed monthly income. We're haggling over terms right now."

"That's wonderful, Ben," she said, almost sincerely. It was terrific to know that Christy might be able to live permanently with her father, but Laura couldn't help wishing Renee had been uncooperative for a little while longer. Laura had been counting on staying married to Ben for at least two years. Now it looked as if their marriage might be over within the month. She wondered what Ben would do if she burst into tears. Probably cope splendidly. He wasn't the sort of man to be thrown off stride by a woman's tears.

But of course she was a sensible, mature adult so she didn't cry. She stretched her mouth into another enthusiastic smile and repeated how wonderful everything was.

Ben smiled back. "This is a real breakthrough, Laura, and it's all thanks to you. Aaron informed Renee the moment you and I were married, and I guess our strategy worked. For the first time that tame shark she calls a lawyer is running scared."

Laura did her best to look deliriously happy. "Then everything's going to be settled much sooner than you expected?"

He paused, glancing toward her with a rather odd intensity. "Well, yes, I guess it is."

"I'm a bit late for work, but if you want to talk about our divorce—"

"No, not now." He stopped, then continued less sharply. "It's much too early for that."

Laura couldn't see why, but she'd already discovered that if you didn't want to hear the answer, it was better not to ask the question. Better not to find out how soon Ben planned to terminate their marriage. Better—much better—to live in a fool's paradise for a little longer, even if paradise only existed at night.

In fact, Laura was becoming positively adept at the mental gymnastics that allowed her to question only what was convenient, and to remember only what she wanted to remember. She was genuinely shocked when Ben reminded her that he would soon be leaving for L.A.

It was on Tuesday night, six days after their wedding, and they had made love with their usual silent intensity. Afterward, Ben lay beside her, staring up at the ceiling. "I'm taking the ten o'clock flight to L.A. on Thursday," he said abruptly. "Shooting on *Empire* started again this week and I have to be there."

For a moment she could scarcely breathe, let alone talk. "Christy will miss you," she said at last, proud of her calm tone.

"I'll get back as soon as I can. The weekend after next for sure."

"Don't worry, Ben, I'll take great care of Christy. She'll be safe with me."

He made no response. A few seconds passed, then he turned toward her, pulling her into his arms and taking her mouth with a swift, hard kiss. "This is to help you remember me when I'm gone," he said.

As if she could possibly forget.

Laura hurried into the parking lot as soon as she got off work on Wednesday afternoon. She was late again. Sometimes she wondered if the criminal underworld had invented a secret system for causing trouble right at the end of a police officer's shift. Today of all days she'd wanted to leave on time.

She got into the car. Four-thirty. That meant she had fifteen minutes to get to her appointment at Christy's school, and she obviously wasn't going to make it. One of the school guidance counselors had called yesterday to arrange a meeting. He wanted to discuss Christy's test scores, which ranged all the way from brilliant to totally abysmal. Christy, perhaps in an effort to deflect her father's ire, had immediately invited Laura to join them at the conference.

Laura headed toward Cherry Creek, dodging stoplights and cursing silently. Her relationship with Christy was the one bright spot in her entire marriage and she didn't want to mess it up. She hoped very much that Christy would understand why she was late, but teenagers had an annoying habit of being unpunctual themselves while expecting adults always to be on time.

She had reached Canyon Street, which meant that the junior high school was only half a mile away. Laura cut across a couple of lanes and managed to get into a faster stream of traffic. She turned into the school parking lot with a sigh of relief. Four-fifty. Five minutes late. It could have been a lot worse.

Locking the door of the Pinto, she searched around in her purse for the directions Christy had written out. *Side entrance A, close to the gym. Main staircase to second floor. Turn left, and it's the third door on your right. Mr. Perkins is my counselor, room 203.*

They would have to remind Mr. Perkins that Christy hadn't taken any formal courses for almost six months, Laura thought, hurrying up the final few stairs to the second floor. Her scores in some subjects had been really good, considering how long it had been since she did any concentrated studying.

A tiny, middle-aged woman stumbled out of an office immediately to Laura's right. She was clutching her head and blood dripped through her fingers, spattering onto her blouse. "The police! Thank God you're here!" she exclaimed, seizing Laura's arm. "I only just put down the phone to the emergency people a couple of minutes ago. It's Scott! You've got to get him, he's up on the roof and drunk as a lord."

"Up on the roof?" Laura repeated quickly. "One of your students?"

"Yes. And there's no safety railing up there. We warned the school board, but they said there were no funds—" She broke off, swaying visibly, until Laura caught her and grasped her around the waist.

"I'm Sergeant Forbes of the Denver police, and I'm here as a parent, not in answer to your call. But you need medical attention. Please let me get you some help."

The counselor slumped against Laura's chest. "No time. He'll fall. Oh, my God, he's only a kid, we've got to reach him!"

They were standing outside room 212. Laura made a

swift decision and half walked, half carried the tiny counselor down the hallway. "How do I get out onto the roof?" she asked tersely.

The counselor roused herself with an effort. "The fire escape next to my office. Scott ran up there when he saw me fall. He was making a few wild threats, but he didn't mean to hurt me. I tripped over the phone cord and banged my head on a filing cabinet." She tried to smile. "That's what happens when you're only five feet tall."

They had arrived at room 203. Laura knocked on the door, opening it without waiting for permission. Ben and Christy were both there, and a man was seated behind the desk, presumably Christy's counselor.

"Sorry to disturb you," she said, "but there's been an accident." Ben happened to be standing closest to the door and she almost pushed the fainting counselor into his astonished arms. "This lady needs medical help right away. There's a kid on the roof and I'm going after him. Don't let anybody else up on the fire escape. The boy's life may depend on keeping him from being scared."

Not waiting for Ben's reply, she sprinted along the hallway and climbed the narrow metal steps of the fire escape at breakneck speed. What was the kid's name? Lord, she couldn't blank out now. Scott. That was it.

The sliding overhead door leading to the roof was open, and Laura slowed her pace as she reached the last few steps of the fire escape. If the boy was as drunk as his counselor implied, she couldn't afford to startle him.

Cautiously she poked her head through the trapdoor and scanned the roof. Yes, there he was, clutching a fifth of vodka, leaning against a chimney and swaying precariously. She'd forgotten to ask the counselor how old he was, but since he was still in junior high, he wasn't likely to be much more than fifteen. However, he looked big enough to be dangerous.

Slowly, quietly, Laura eased herself through the door

and immediately sat down. Police uniforms could be intimidating. "Hi, Scott," she said quietly. "Your counselor sent me. I've come to help you get back inside."

"You arresting me?"

"No." She made her answer unequivocal. She didn't want him panicked and, anyway, she'd prefer to avoid arresting him if she could.

"Then push off," he said, taking another swig from the bottle. "I like it up here."

"It won't be much fun once it gets dark." Laura rose carefully to her feet. No reaction from Scott. She took a single step toward him. Still no reaction. He was too drunk to be observant. She spoke coaxingly. "If you came inside, maybe we could talk things over."

"Nothin' to talk about, police lady. I'm staying up here for a while and when I get good and ready I'm gonna take me a little walk over the edge. I wanna see how it feels to fly."

The chimney was no more than seven feet from the edge of the roof. If Scott took even a couple of careless steps backward, in his drunken state he might not be able to keep his balance. He would fly all right—for about five seconds.

"There are a lot of people who'd be very unhappy if you did that, Scott." Her shirt was clinging to her back with sweat as she edged closer to the chimney. "Your friends, your teachers at this school. I'm sure there are a lot of people who care about you, Scott."

"What about my parents, police lady? Don't forget to tell me how sorry they'll be when I'm gone."

He's having problems with his parents. The thought flashed with lightning speed into Laura's brain. "Whatever you may think right now, Scott, I'm sure your parents would be very sorry." She took another step toward the chimney. Three more and she'd be there.

"Sure, my dad would be real sorry. That's why he lit

out of town twelve years ago, because he loved me so much."

Laura flinched as Scott slammed the vodka bottle into the chimney, breaking it in half. He brandished the jagged neck in front of him. "Don't you come no closer," he said. "I can see what you're trying to do. Stay right where you are, police lady."

In the distance, not too far away, she could hear the sound of sirens. Dear God, if only she could keep him safe until the rescue squad arrived!

"I need to sit down," she said, hoping he was too drunk to notice the fear in her voice. "It's been a long day, and I'm tired. I'd like to rest my back against that chimney."

"Don't do it, lady!" he screamed, but his hand holding the broken bottle trembled and he made no other move to stop her.

She took the final step and clung to the chimney for a moment, shaking with relief. She used her foot to clear a patch of roof free from shards of broken bottle.

"What's bothering you, Scott?" she asked quietly, sitting down and leaning her back against the chimney. The less threatening she appeared, the greater her chances of getting through to him.

He grunted, floundering drunkenly as he swung around to confront her. Laura held her breath when he moved, but he ended up at least three feet farther away from the edge of the roof. Three feet closer to safety.

"My sex life ain't living up to expectations," he said with deliberate crudity. "That's what's bothering me. How about you, police lady?"

"I've just moved to a new house," she said, ignoring his innuendo. "How about you, Scott? Have you always lived in Denver?"

"One place or another. Dependin' on how far behind we were in the rent. Mom wasn't real good at paying the bills."

"Your mother probably had a hard time if your father didn't help her at all. It isn't easy for a woman to make enough to support a family."

He laughed harshly. "Don't worry, she ain't got no more problems, police lady. She's got herself a brand-new house and a brand-new husband to go with it. Trouble is, my brand-new dad decided he didn't want me in their nice neat house. Last weekend he told me to get out and stay out."

Laura felt a sudden weariness. Sometimes she really got tired of hearing the same sad story over and over again. But the sirens were getting closer now, and this wasn't the moment to relax her concentration. She could hear the unmistakable sounds of the emergency vehicles screeching to a halt in the parking lot below. She needed to distract Scott's attention while the rescue squad got ladders and other equipment into position.

"There are people who can help you, Scott." She got to her feet, every nerve on the alert. "The counselors in this school, maybe, or some more social workers if the situation seems too tough for the school to handle. You'd be surprised how even the worst family problems can be worked out when you have professional help."

Way down in the parking lot, some idiot with a bull-horn shouted out an order to stand clear for the firemen. Scott whirled around, his eyes rolling white with panic. "They ain't gonna lock me up," he said to Laura. "They ain't gonna do that to me."

He broke into a run, lurching from side to side in his effort to stay upright on the uneven surface of the roof. Laura ran after him, catching him easily and holding him in a lightly applied half nelson. She tossed the broken bottle to the far end of the roof.

But Scott was strong, and desperation gave him cunning. He twisted out of Laura's grip and dashed toward his delusion of freedom—the side of the roof.

She caught up with him less than two feet from the

edge, pulling him back to safety by the simple device of falling in toward the center and taking him with her. As soon as she recovered her breath, she rolled him face down on the asphalt and handcuffed his wrists behind him. The idiot with the bullhorn was still shouting out orders, but now she could also hear the reassuring sounds of people climbing ladders.

"Sorry, Scott, but I'm not going to let you die just because you're feeling sorry for yourself. Somebody will contact your mother, and tomorrow morning the world's going to look a much brighter place. I guarantee it."

He sat up, watching sullenly as a half dozen firemen arrived simultaneously on the roof.

Laura stood up, dusting dead leaves and bits of gravel from her uniform. "He needs a doctor and a social worker," she said quietly to the first fireman who reached their side.

"You okay, Officer?" the fireman asked. "From what we could see down there, it looked like you were having some trouble."

"I'm fine. Or I will be when I've had a bath." Scott was having a safety harness fixed around him by one of the firemen and she touched him very lightly on the arm.

"Take care," she said. "I hope things work out for you."

He didn't look at her until he was at the head of the fire escape. Then he turned around. "I didn't really wanna die," he said. "Thanks, lady."

Her legs were shaking so much that she needed help down the fire escape. Once in the main school building, she accepted a plastic cup of water and asked what had happened to the wounded counselor.

"She's with the paramedics now," a fireman replied. "She's doing fine."

"And my husband? He and my daughter were in another counselor's office when I went up onto the roof."

"The principal cleared the building, miss. He's probably waiting for you outside."

Laura fought her way through a phalanx of police, rescue workers, and the usual crowd of bystanders. She'd no sooner passed through the police cordon than Ben was there, sweeping her into his arms and crushing her against his chest.

"Oh, my God, Laura, are you all right? You didn't get hurt? I've been going crazy ever since I saw you dash up onto the roof. I tried to follow you, but we had to take care of the injured counselor and by the time we found a nurse, the school principal insisted on clearing the building."

"I'm fine, except I'm hot and dirty and feeling sorry for that poor kid."

"Sorry for him! Dear God, Laura, I love you so much, and when I saw you up there on the roof, confronting that crazy kid with his broken bottle, I suddenly realized what a total, damned fool I've been in refusing to admit how I felt. I love you, Laura. I feel like I need to say it a million times."

Laura let out a sigh of supreme contentment and melted against him. His mouth seized hers, sealing her lips with an endless kiss. She let her eyes drift closed, listening blissfully to his feverish endearments.

When he finally stopped kissing her, she cupped his face between her still-dusty hands and nuzzled his cheek. "I love you, too," she said softly. "But I think you probably know that."

He grinned down at her. "I think half the United States will know it soon."

"What do you mean?" She stared at him, then blinked as he swiveled her around, still holding her tightly within the circle of his arms.

Laura swallowed—hard. She and Ben were eyeball

to eyeball with no less than five separate TV cameras, which, she realized, must have been sent to the school in the wake of the rescue squad.

"Do you think we provided them with some interesting footage?" Ben asked, smiling at her horrified expression.

Five determined reporters, microphones in hand, pressed forward, demanding a statement. By coincidence—Laura wasn't sure whether it was good or bad—Tessa Renier happened to be the Channel 8 representative on the scene.

"Well, well, well," she said, looking from Ben to Laura with undisguised satisfaction. "And to think I complained about being sent out on a rinky-dink story." She extended the microphone. "It's a pleasure to meet you again, Ms. Forbes. The last time we saw each other in Vail, Ben explained that you and he were *just good friends*. Do you have any additions or alterations you'd like to make to that statement?"

Before Laura could speak, Ben took her hand and raised it to his lips. "Laura and I are still the best of friends," he said softly. "But for the past week we happen to have been married as well."

For a split second Tess and the other reporters were stunned into silence, then the normal journalistic instincts returned and the babble of questions began.

Veteran of a hundred interviews, Ben fielded most of the questions with casual grace. After about ten minutes, he called a halt. "My wife has just spent a grueling half hour preventing a dangerous young man from jumping off a roof. As you can see, she's exhausted. It's time for us to get home."

Politely but firmly, he shouldered his way past the TV cameras and the press crews, keeping Laura close to his side.

Her addled brain finally started functioning again when they reached the relative peace and quiet of the front of the school. "Where's Christy?" she asked. "I'm sure I saw her with you in the counselor's office."

"The principal asked a teacher to drive her home. He didn't think it was a good idea for Christy to watch you grapple with a young classmate bent on suicide. As soon as the firemen took Scott into custody, I called home to let her know you were safe."

He opened the passenger door to the Mercedes. "Hop in," he said. "We'll soon be home."

Laura paused with one foot inside the car. "The Pinto! I just remembered it's in the other parking lot."

"I'll send Juan to pick it up tomorrow. Get into the car, honey. You're asleep on your feet."

"There are moments when bossy husbands have their advantages," she admitted, getting into the car and slumping against the leather upholstery. She yawned. "You can wake me up *after* I've had a shower. I'm too tired to do anything difficult like washing myself."

Ben grinned. "Sounds like a situation with interesting possibilities."

"Only if you're a man who's turned on by comatose bodies."

Laura was, in truth, less than half-awake by the time they arrived back at the house, but Christy's enthusiastic hugs soon revived her. "You're a heroine!" she exclaimed, dancing excitedly around the hallway. "My mother the heroine! And the best of it is, Dad was so worried about you he forgot to complain about my test scores."

"Well, now that I've remembered . . ." Ben advanced toward her threateningly.

She laughed, then adjusted her face into an expression of mock piety. "You don't have to say another word, Dad, I'm off to my room to study. Again."

He frowned. "Are you sick? What's this sudden unnatural fascination with homework?"

Christy grinned mischievously. "No fascination at

all. It's just an excuse. I decided it would be kind of neat to have a baby brother or sister some time in the near future, and I'd like you two to have plenty of chance to work on the project. Neither of you is getting any younger, you know."

Ben glanced uncertainly toward his wife, for once in his life at a loss for words.

Laura smiled at him serenely. "Sometimes your daughter has the most terrific ideas."

Chapter Twelve

BEN DEMONSTRATED, WITH amazing thoroughness, that an oversized bathtub had many uses other than rinsing away rooftop grime, and Laura discovered that fatigue could mysteriously vanish in the midst of hectic activity.

When he had finished washing her, a task that seemed to have little to do with soap or washcloths and a great deal to do with trailing bubbles over her body and then kissing her until they disappeared, he wrapped her in a giant bathtowel and carried her to their bed.

He opened the towel, his fingers stroking her skin, touching her breasts and drifting down to the flat planes of her stomach. "Next time," he said with pretended arrogance, "before you get up on a roof to rescue some crazy carrying a broken bottle, you're to ask my permission."

She saw the hint of genuine fear in his eyes and wriggled against him with deliberate provocation. "Darling, I love it when you do your Harrison Brand impersonation. It's so *exciting*."

178

"Is it?" he said, with a touch of grimness. His mouth came down hard on hers, but she met his kiss eagerly and after a few seconds she felt the anger leave him. He groaned against her mouth, his kiss gentling, and when he lifted his head, remorse gleamed briefly in his eyes.

"My job isn't usually dangerous," she said softly.

"Often enough," he replied, capturing her hands and holding them against the pillows. "I can see there's no hope for it. I'll have to keep you barefoot and pregnant and then they'll throw you off the force." Holding her wrists with one hand, he trailed his other hand down to her breast and stroked lazy circles around her nipple. He watched with undisguised satisfaction as the newly erect nipple thrust against his palm. "What do you think of that idea, Ms. Police Person?"

She simply smiled and slid down the bed as far as her pinioned hands would allow. It was far enough. She pressed a taunting, openmouthed kiss against his chest, her eyes gleaming with silent laughter when she felt him shiver. "I think the pregnant part sounds wonderful," she whispered. "But I'd prefer to wear shoes."

He dragged her up the bed until he could reach her mouth, kissing her with an explosion of pent-up need. His mouth plundered hers remorselessly and his hands explored her body with heated urgency. With each restless movement he spiraled her passion higher, until she trembled helplessly within the circle of his arms.

Ben looked down at her, his eyes glittering, his face a taut mask of desire. "I love you," he said hoarsely. "I've wanted to say that to you every time we made love. I don't know why it seemed so difficult to say the words."

"I love you, too."

Her body blazed into exultant life, and she exploded into the world of wild joy where only Ben could take her, shattering into a million shimmering pieces as he clung to her and murmured her name.

Later, a long time later, they sat up in bed munching roast beef sandwiches.

Laura propped herself up against a stack of pillows and sighed contentedly. "Now I know why my mother always told me I should marry a rich man. She must have known that rich men have housekeepers who leave roast beef sandwiches ready made in the refrigerator."

Ben smiled lazily. "I know your mother too well to fall for that story. I'm sure she always told you to marry for love." He reached for the television's remote control unit. "Want to see yourself being a heroine on TV? The late-night news has already started."

He flipped to Channel 8, which was broadcasting an advertisement for toothpaste. This, in turn, was followed by pictures of a warehouse going up in flames. The warehouse having been pictorially reduced to rubble, the newscaster smiled toothily into the camera.

"Another potentially tragic story had a happy ending this evening. A young man was rescued from the roof of Cherry Hills Junior High School by Police Sergeant Laura Forbes of the Denver police."

A shot, obviously taken by telephoto lens, showed Laura subduing Scott on the rooftop and throwing away his broken bottle. The voice of the newscaster overrode the pictures. "Ms. Forbes, however, is more than just a brave policewoman. As Tessa Renier, our reporter on the spot discovered, she is also the wife of a very famous man."

The brightly lit studio scene was replaced by a crowded view of the school parking lot. Laura stared in undisguised fascination as Ben, looking at his most rakish, broke through the police cordon and dragged Laura into his arms. Their kiss, Laura thought, torn between acute embarrassment and secret pride, made most of Harrison Brand's efforts look tame by comparison.

In a rare display of good taste, the editors had blocked out the original sound track and substituted a voice-over of the reporter explaining that Laura Forbes, Denver police officer, and Bennett Logan, star of television's number-one-rated show, had been married recently in a private ceremony.

Their kiss—their endless kiss—finally faded into another commercial and Ben flipped off the set. He took Laura into his arms, smiling teasingly. "There's no doubt about it, Mrs. Logan, you're turning into a fine performer. Definite star quality, I'd say. But if you want a part in my next production, I'll need to see if you can duplicate that fine performance we just saw on the screen." He patted the bed. "Fortunately you can audition right here."

She fluttered her eyelashes. "Mr. Logan, are you suggesting I have to bribe you with my luscious body to get a part in your movie?"

He kissed the tip of her nose. "Every actor has to sacrifice for his art. You don't see me complaining." He nuzzled the pulse beating in the hollow of her throat. "Well, Mrs. Logan, does this seem a good place to begin your sacrifice?"

"No," she said, pulling his mouth down to meet her own. "Personally, I think we ought to begin right here."